Arcane Awakenings
Books One and Two

Shelley Russell Nolan

Creator: Nolan, Shelley Russell, author.
Title: Arcane Awakenings Books One and Two / Shelley Russell Nolan
ISBN: 978-0-6481683-1-7

Subjects: Fantasy fiction

Printed in Australia by Ingram Spark
Cover design: Mariah Sinclair

www.shelleyrussellnolan.com

Also by Shelley Russell Nolan

Lost Reaper
(Book One of the Reaper Series)

Winged Reaper
(Book Two of the Reaper Series)

Silver Reaper
(Book Three of the Reaper Series)

For Donna

Contents

Book One

Angel Fire

1

I stared at the little blue pill in the palm of my hand.

Tired of waking coated in sweat, with the bed sheets twisted around my legs, I'd grabbed the last packet of pills out of the top drawer of my bedside table, despairing that the months spent weaning myself off the medication had been for nothing.

The pill, innocuous and yet seductive, promised a dreamless night and a return to existing on autopilot.

My hand shook as I lifted it toward my mouth, the sting of failure making my eyes water. Aunt Joyce had predicted I wouldn't be able to handle life without medication and would snap under the pressure of the real world. The day I moved out she'd stood in the doorway and watched me pile my bags into the back of the taxi, as usual making no attempt to hide her scorn.

She'd said I wouldn't last six months without medication.

If I swallowed this pill, I'd be proving her right.

My spine stiffened, and I made a fist.

No.

She was the one who was wrong.

I launched myself off the bed and raced to the toilet. Before I could think twice, I lifted the lid and threw the pill into the bowl. Breathing ragged, I flushed the toilet, and watched the water carry temptation away.

Sweat trickled down my forehead, and I wiped it away with the back of my hand as I returned to my room. I sat on the edge of the bed, hunched over, arms wrapped around my stomach as I rocked backward and forward. Gradually my breathing eased, and I lay down, arms at my sides, hands gripping the sheet beneath me. I stared at the ceiling, at the shadows cast by the lamp on the bedside table.

Eyelids impossibly heavy, given weight by weeks of disturbed nights, they closed, and sleep claimed me.

It felt as if I'd only just fallen asleep when I was transported to the room that had haunted me for as long as I could remember.

I stand in the open doorway as the empty room ripples before filling with furniture. Twin timber beds rest against one wall, covered in matching pink quilts with a colourful collection of stuffed toys on the pillows. White lace billows over the window between the beds and glittering fairies dance on the pink and white curtains hanging open on either side.

On the opposite side of the room a brown rocking horse with a golden mane sits beside a large pink and white toy box. An ornate dollhouse rests on a multi-coloured rug in the centre of the room, just waiting to be played with by little hands.

The room is neat and tidy, everything in its place, but I know that will soon change. My stomach clenches, dread filling my mouth with bile. I struggle to move, to leave the room, but remain frozen in place, helpless to do anything but bear witness as the dream plays out before me.

The room ripples, and now it is no longer neat. Toys are strewn over the floor, the quilts have been thrown off the beds, and the sheets rumpled. A small child sits on one of the beds, legs dangling over the edge. She is beautiful, with dark blonde curls and sleepy indigo eyes, one chubby hand clutching a well-worn teddy to her chest. She appears to be around three years of age.

The little girl is me, a reflection of the child I had once been. I smile at my former self, enjoying this moment of peace even though I know it is not to last. The room ripples once more and I shudder as the dream shifts to nightmare.

The room goes dark and smoke obscures my vision. I wave a hand in front of my face to clear the smoke away, and desperately search for the little girl. She is now standing in the middle of the bed, beseeching me with terror-filled eyes.

A crackling noise from behind makes me spin around and I find myself looking down a long hall filled with smoke, flames licking the walls, heat pressing against my face. Mesmerised by the flames, my attention is caught, until a terrified scream has me turning back to my childhood self.

Fire is devouring the fairies on the curtains as the little girl backs away from them in fear. She reaches the end of the bed and looks over her shoulder at me.

'Help me, Andie, please. I'm scared.' The little girl stretches a hand toward me. Her mouth doesn't move, but her words echo in my head.

I want to take her in my arms and pluck her to safety. I take one step inside the room, jumping back when part of the ceiling collapses to the floor in front of me, crushing the dollhouse. I move around it, one hand shielding my eyes when the rug beneath the chunk of ceiling catches fire. Heat blasts me from all sides as the little girl silently cries my name. I reach out to her and she smiles as our fingertips touch. I lean forward, preparing to take the last step so I can scoop her into my arms.

Something grabs me around my waist and pulls me back.

'No.' I struggle to break free, striving with all my might to go to the little girl, hoping this time the unseen force will relent.

'Andie!' The little girl screams, retreating to the other end of the bed as more of the ceiling caves in between us.

'Let me go.' Tears stream down my cheeks. I desperately want to go back, to rescue the little girl. Instead, I am picked *up and carried down the hall.*

The child's cries get louder, more insistent, and I cover my ears but am unable to block them out as they are inside my head. Smoke fills my lungs and I choke on it, eyes stinging and chest heaving.

Then darkness takes me.

I bolted upright, coughing, rubbing my abraded throat, an echo of the little girl's screams ringing in my ears. My body trembled as an acute sense of loss filled me. Shivers racked my body and I grabbed a throw rug off the end of the bed and wrapped it around my shoulders in a vain effort to get warm. A wide yawn made my eyes water but I resisted the urge to lie down. Even if I did manage to go back to sleep, experience taught me the nightmare would return.

I grabbed my mobile phone off the bedside table and checked the time. Three am. I stared at the wall opposite my bed, still seeing the little girl's face, my face. I rubbed my eyes, wiping away tears, wishing I knew why this dream continued to haunt me.

The first time had been the night after my parents died in a car accident. All I had were vague memories of waking in the middle of the night, in a strange room, screaming. I'd called for my mum, only to be told she was gone and Joyce, Uncle Bill's new wife, was now my mother. A woman I had never met stood beside the bed, frowning at me. Then she walked out of the room without saying another word, leaving it to my older brother Daniel to comfort me.

The next morning, she and Uncle Bill took me to see a psychiatrist, who explained away my nightmare as a reaction to the changes in my environment and the trauma of losing my parents. It would go away once I'd settled in at my new home, the shrink said. But the dreams didn't go away, they got worse, and five shrinks later Aunt Joyce found one who said sedatives were the answer.

Every night, for the next fifteen years, my aunt would appear with a glass of water in one gloved hand and my dose in the other. She'd pry my mouth open and toss the pill into the back of my throat. Then she'd hold my mouth shut, grab hold of my hair and wrench my head back until I swallowed. Only then would I be allowed to take a sip of water. The nightly ritual never changed, and I learned early on that my tears and childish pleas were useless.

The dosage increased year by year and by the time I turned thirteen it had reached a level where it became impossible for me to shake off the effects the next day. Thoughts dull, unable to fully engage with the people around me, I muddled my way through high school, hiding out in the library during breaks.

Daniel was my only friend, my confidante, my lifeline. I would have gone crazy for real if he wasn't there to support me. Then he finished his apprenticeship as an electrician and moved out. Though he regularly came to visit, it was not the same. I was essentially alone, imprisoned in a body that did not feel as if it belonged to me, with Aunt Joyce hovering in the background ready to shove even more pills down my throat.

When I turned eighteen, legally an adult, I'd packed my bags and caught a taxi to Daniel's flat. His flatmate had found living away from home too expensive and returned to his parents a month earlier, leaving Daniel to cover the full cost of the rent. Most brothers wouldn't be keen on having their little sister moving in, but Daniel knew how much I hated living at Bill and Joyce's without him, and so far, it seemed to be working out.

I was halfway through my first year at Easton University, studying nursing while working part-time at a local nursing home. My income, along with the subsidy I received from the government, covered my share of the rent and kept me fed. There wasn't much left in the bank once the bills had been paid each week, but I was happy to forgo new clothes or nights out to escape my aunt's religious adherence to perfection.

I was the antithesis of perfection.

Aunt Joyce was not able to hide her relief when I announced I was leaving home, a far cry from the reaction Daniel had received a year earlier. But then, he'd never caused her sleepless nights or needed expensive medical treatment. Though it was never said aloud, I knew she and Uncle Bill regretted their decision to adopt me formally. If they weren't focused on keeping up the appearance of the perfect family, I'm sure they would have sent me away and just kept Daniel.

I sighed, shaking my head to banish such gloomy thoughts, and reached for the book on my bedside table. I was keen to lose myself in someone else's life for a while. I'd just finished the first chapter when a bang set my heart racing.

I let the book fall to the bed and tossed the throw rug aside as I got to my feet.

'Daniel, is that you?' I wrenched open my bedroom door and stepped out into the hall as another bang, followed by the sound of breaking glass, came from the kitchen. I sped down the hall and skidded to a stop when I saw Daniel standing in front of the sink. His left hand was held up in front of him, blood pooling in the centre of his palm.

'Oh my God, what happened?' I made my way to his side, skirting the broken glass on the floor.

He blinked at me, body swaying, eyes bloodshot.

I frowned. 'Have you been drinking?' This was not like Daniel. He was usually so serious; he hardly ever had more than two beers.

'I dropped a glass,' he said, slurring his words as he held

his palm up for me to inspect.

'I see that.' I took his hand and ran it under the cold tap to rinse off the blood. A jagged piece of glass was embedded in his palm and I prised it free, pleased to see it left only a small cut. I grabbed a tea towel and wrapped it around his hand, then led him around the broken glass and over to the small dining table tucked into a corner of the kitchen.

'I tried to clean it up,' he said, pointing to the dustpan and brush he had pulled out of the cupboard under the sink.

'It's okay, I'll take care of it.' I made him sit down and manoeuvred him around until his uninjured hand rested on top of his injured one. 'But first I need to take care of you. Hold that while I get the first aid kit.'

He gave me a bleary smile and nodded, slumping down in the chair until his chin was sitting on his chest.

I got the first aid kit from the bathroom and ran back to the kitchen.

Daniel was no longer sitting at the table. I searched through the flat and found him lying face down on his bed, snoring softly, left arm trailing over the side. He didn't move as I undid the tea towel and wiped the puncture wound with an antiseptic cloth. Once the area was dry, I placed a dressing over it and smoothed it in place.

He was so out of it he didn't make a sound as I placed his arm back on the bed. Then I packed up the first aid kit and stashed it away in the bathroom cupboard. Back in the kitchen, I grabbed the dustpan and brush and made quick work of the mess he'd made.

Daniel's behaviour was so out of character; something had to be seriously wrong. My stomach clenched at the thought.

He was all I had.

I couldn't lose him.

2

I tossed the broken glass into the rubbish bin and put the dustpan and brush away, brow creasing when I heard a strange noise. It sounded almost like someone crying, and it was coming from Daniel's room. Eyebrows raised, I tiptoed down the hall and peered into his bedroom.

Daniel still lay on his bed, only he was now curled up on his side with his back to me. Sobs racked his body and I crept further into the room, hesitant to intrude yet wanting to help. I got close enough to touch him, and could see he was clutching something to his chest.

I stretched out my hand, reaching for his shoulder.

'Angel,' he said.

Startled, I jumped back, letting out a soft squeal and smothering it with my hand.

'I'm so sorry. It's all my fault,' he said, and started murmuring the same name repeatedly. 'Angel.'

Goosebumps covered my body at the anguish in his voice. I rubbed my arms, shivering in the cool morning air, as I leaned over him. His eyes were closed, and he didn't react when I squeezed his shoulder. But with my touch his breathing eased, and the murmuring stopped.

I straightened up, relief swamping me at a mundane explanation for his out of character behaviour. This Angel must be his girlfriend and they were going through a break-up. Not that he'd ever seemed serious about any of the girls that showed up from time to time. Tall and fit, with the same indigo coloured eyes as me, teamed with light brown hair, he attracted them without even trying, but I didn't think I'd ever heard him mention a girl named Angel before.

Should I wake him, and see if he wanted to talk about it?

No, better to wait and ask him about it in the morning, when he wouldn't be embarrassed to have his little sister find him crying drunk over a girl. I went back to my room, lay on the bed and closed my eyes, vainly hoping this time my sleep would be dream-free.

When the first ripple subsides, instead of a child's bedroom, I am surrounded by trees, moonlight creating dappled shadows on the grass at my feet. Through gaps in the trees I see a high mesh fence with a large sign hanging from it. I walk toward it, getting close enough to see it is a danger sign for an electric fence. I stop walking and stare at the sign, puzzled by its appearance in my dream.

A soft voice calls my name and a second later I hear running footsteps behind me.

I spin around. A young woman dressed in a long white nightgown runs toward me. Barefoot and with dark blonde hair flowing behind her, she emerges from the shadows cast by the trees surrounding us, enveloped in a golden glow.

I stop breathing, time standing still as she halts in front of me, staring at me with my own eyes. The vision smiles, her expression joyous. I smile back, marvelling at the replica my dreaming mind has created, though there are subtle differences. The vision has hair that hangs below her waist in gentle curls, while mine falls halfway down my back and I have a side swept fringe. But our faces are exactly the same.

The vision steps forward and takes my hand. 'Andie, help me.'

It is eerie to hear my name, in my voice, coming from a vision whose mouth doesn't move, but at the same time it feels so familiar, like something I've experienced hundreds of times before.

I shake my head, pushing my confusion away to focus on the vision's plea for help. 'What do you want me to do?'

'I need you to come and find me, Andie. They're hurting me. Please, you have to find me, and make them stop.' Tears form in her eyes, the hand holding mine gripping tight.

'Who is hurting you?' Though I know this is a dream, the desperation in her eyes has me longing to make her fear go away.

'They are.' The vision points back the way she came, and I can just make out several figures running through the trees in the distance, torchlight flickering as they search.

Sounds drift in the still night air, and I hear voices calling, still too far away to make out the words. I strain my ears, listening carefully, and gasp as what I hear sinks in.

They are calling for Angel.

The fear in the vision's eyes intensifies and she squeezes my hand. 'Please hurry, Andie. I need you. Help me.'

Her form wavers, though she clings to my hand so hard it hurts, and soon I can see through her. Then she vanishes, leaving me with four half-moon shaped indents in the back of my hand.

Heart pounding, I opened my eyes, still seeing the vision's terrified face, my terrified face. I pulled the quilt up to my chin to ward off the sudden chill that gripped me.

Where had this new dream come from? Had it been triggered by Daniel's mention of someone called Angel?

The burgeoning dawn sent gentle light through the open window and I reached over to turn off the lamp on my bedside table, wincing as the movement caused pain to flare on the back of my right hand. I held it in front of me and stared in shock at the four distinct nail marks, just like the ones from my dream.

Had I made the marks in my sleep, causing me to then

dream about it happening? It was the only explanation that made sense, and yet it seemed impossible I could do that to myself while I was asleep.

A voice sounded in my head. 'Help me, Andie. Please, save me.'

I launched off the bed, pulse racing as I scanned the room. I backed up to the wall and switched on the light. Brightness flooded the room, dispelling the shadows but doing nothing to calm my thoughts. I was wide awake, alone in my room, hearing voices. A strange current moved over my skin, wrapping around me before flitting away, and the hairs on my arms rose.

I wrenched open my door and bolted down the hall to Daniel's room. He was fast asleep, lying on his back, one hand holding something on his chest. I wanted to wake him, to have him reassure me I wasn't going crazy, that a voice, my voice, hadn't just spoken to me in my room, to explain away the marks on my hand.

I put a hand on his shoulder, ready to shake him, but hesitated. If I told him what had happened he'd be sure to mention it to Bill and Joyce the next time he spoke to them. They would be quick to take it as another sign of my inadequacy. Joyce would ramp up her campaign to get me back on my medication, and maybe this time Daniel would side with them.

I couldn't bear it if he started to look at me with disappointment in his eyes too.

Maybe I had imagined the voice, the dream affecting me more than I'd thought. I rubbed my arms and gazed at Daniel, torn over what I should do, fear this was some kind of mental snap freezing me in place.

I was not going crazy. I wasn't.

I leaned over Daniel, needing to talk to him, to tell him what had happened, even if it might lead him to think I was crazy. My fear gave way to curiosity when I realised the item he was clutching to his chest was a photograph.

Was it a picture of his girlfriend, this mysterious Angel?

I peered down at it, but the bulk of it was obscured by his hand and all I could see was part of the background. After checking to see if he was still fast asleep, I carefully prised the photo out from under his fingers. I held it up to the sliver of light coming through a gap in his curtains.

My knees buckled, and I gripped the bedhead to stop myself from toppling over.

Identical twin girls with dark blonde curls and indigo eyes smiled up at me. A caption beneath the photo read 'Andrea and Angela, 3yrs and 5 months' and below that was the date the photo had been taken, fifteen years ago.

3

I stumbled out of Daniel's room and retreated to my own, unable to tear my eyes away from the proof I had a twin sister.

Where was she?

Why had no one told me she existed?

How could I have forgotten my own twin?

Hands shaking, I sat on my bed, tears falling on the photo. I hadn't forgotten, not completely. My recurring dreams had shown me what I'd lost.

Angela was Angel.

Anger swamped me, burning away my tears. My aunt and uncle had dragged me to countless psychiatric sessions, forced me to take medication I didn't need, all of it designed to wipe away any memory of my twin.

I clapped a hand over my mouth.

The fire.

That must have been how Angel died. That was what my dreams had been trying to tell me, to make me remember. She had been trapped in a burning room, screaming for me to save her, and I'd left her there to die.

Pain tore through me and I gasped for air, hunched over, sobbing for everything I had lost.

An eternity passed before I managed to stifle my sobs. I lay curled up on the bed, staring at the photo, running my fingers over the smiling faces of Angel and me. Why couldn't I remember her and our time together? Why had Daniel kept it from me, robbing me of the chance to mourn her?

As horrible as it was, I could understand why Joyce had

never said anything. It was just like her to pretend Angel never existed. Bad enough that she'd had her seemingly perfect life turned around when our parents died and caring for us had fallen to Bill and her. To have another tragedy linked to the family name would be something she would prefer to keep quiet about.

But Daniel?

He was my brother.

Our brother.

For him to have stood by all these years and not told me about Angel, was wrong on so many levels it twisted my stomach just thinking about it.

When I heard him get out of bed and stumble into the bathroom, I stood. It was time for answers. I marched down the hall and waited outside the bathroom door, tapping my feet as I waited for him to emerge. As soon as he opened the door I thrust the photo in front of his bloodshot eyes.

'Why didn't you tell me I had a twin sister?'

The colour leached from his face. 'Where did you get that? Have you been going through my things?'

'As if that matters. I had a twin sister, and no one told me. How could you do that? How could you pretend you didn't know what was going on, why I was having the same dream night after night? She died in a fire, didn't she?'

He nodded, holding on to the door jamb, a queasy look on his face. 'I'm sorry. I wanted to tell you, but everyone said it was best not to.'

'Everyone, or just Bill and Joyce?'

His brow creased, and he straightened up. 'I wish you wouldn't call them that. You know they don't like it.'

I stifled a snort, and shook my head. 'Unbelievable. They've had you lying to me for fifteen years, and you're still defending them.'

'They took us in when Mum and Dad died, gave us a

home. They were just trying to do the right thing.'

'By turning me into a freak show? Shoving pills down my throat?' I turned away, disgusted by the hurt in his eyes.

'Andie, wait. Let me explain.' He grabbed my arm and spun me around. 'It wasn't like that. After the fire, you were confused. You'd blocked out the memories. It was the experts who advised Mum and Dad to let you continue to forget Angel.'

'They are not our parents. They only agreed to adopt us because there was nowhere else for us to go after Mum and Dad died in the car accident.' He dropped his eyes and my stomach churned. 'Please don't tell me that was a lie.'

He gave a sigh. 'They died in the fire, with Angel. Mum and … Uncle Bill and Aunt Joyce said it would be better if you thought they'd died in a car accident, in case the mention of a fire triggered memories of what really happened.'

I sank to the floor, back against the wall, eyes wide and unseeing. 'This can't be happening. This can't be real.' Horror choked off my voice. This was worse than any nightmare.

Daniel crouched in front of me, reaching out to pull me into his arms.

'No.' I pushed his hands away and scrambled to my feet, breath coming in gasps. 'You do not get to touch me.' Hands clenched into fists, I backed away from him.

'Andie, please, I feel bad enough as it is. Don't shut me out.'

He did look wretched, but I was beyond feeling pity for him. 'What else haven't you told me? What other lies have I been fed?'

His expression became even more pitiful. 'It was my fault Angel died.'

My mouth fell open. 'You set the fire?'

'No, it was caused by an electrical fault. By the time the

smoke alarms went off, half the house was in flames. Mum and Dad were trapped in their bedroom and they yelled at me to get you and Angel out of the house. But I could only carry one of you at a time. I grabbed you first. I swear I was going to go straight back for Angel, but the roof collapsed, and I couldn't get back in the house. But if I'd been stronger, faster, I could have saved her.' Anguish filled his eyes and tears streamed down his cheeks. 'It's my fault she died. I should have been able to save her.'

My anger evaporated, shoulders slumping as I leaned into the wall for support. 'You were a little boy. You can't blame yourself for what happened.'

He shook his head, wiping his eyes with the back of one hand. Then he held it up in front of him, staring at the dressing in confusion.

'You broke a glass, and got a piece of it stuck in your palm,' I said. 'Don't you remember?'

He shrugged. 'I'm not sure. It's all a bit fuzzy. Guess I drank too much.'

'I thought you must have broken up with a girl called Angel. You were crying and saying her name over and over again.'

His strange behaviour had been the trigger for the latest dream. Was it the ghost of Angel's memory, hidden in my subconscious, which made me think I'd heard her voice? I looked at my hand, to see the nail marks had vanished. Had I dreamed them too?

'Yesterday was the anniversary of the fire,' said Daniel, the anguish in his voice dragging my gaze back up to his.

Tears glistened in his eyes. 'I got carried away trying to block out the memories. I envied you, being able to forget. I'll always remember the look on her face as I carried you away, leaving her to die. I know most people didn't think she understood what was going on, but she knew. I could see it in her eyes.'

'What do you mean?'

He wiped his eyes on the sleeve of his shirt. 'Angel was different. She was always doing weird stuff, freaking people out, and she was mute.'

'Mute?'

'She couldn't talk or make any sounds. The doctors never knew why. Mum and Dad said it was because she was special, and started calling her Angel instead of Angela.' His mouth formed a crooked smile. 'You used to do all the talking for her, act as her translator, although you always insisted she could talk. You said you could hear her voice in your head and couldn't understand why we couldn't hear it too.'

I sucked in a breath. In every one of my dreams I'd heard Angel's voice, but her lips hadn't moved. Fifteen years of dreams, in which my subconscious had fought so hard to make me remember her. The job made harder by the medication I'd been forced to take.

All for nothing.

The pills that turned me into a robot, the countless hours spent having my head examined and my dream dissected, none of it made any difference because it had all been based on lies. Had any of the shrinks Bill and Joyce took me to known the truth or had they been lied to as well?

A bitter taste flooded my mouth, not unlike the aftertaste of the pills I'd been forced to swallow for all the wrong reasons.

I bolted into my bedroom, wrenched open the top drawer of my bedside table and pulled out the packet of pills I'd kept hidden away as a safety net.

Daniel followed me, and I thrust the packet into his hand, forcing him to take it.

'Fifteen years these stupid things have ruled my life, making me feel like a failure, that there was something wrong with me, and you knew it was all a lie.' Eyes stinging, I glared at him. 'Why didn't you tell me the truth? How could you stand back and let them do this to me when you knew I wasn't crazy?'

He ran a hand through his hair, sorrow in his eyes. 'I'm so sorry, Andie. They said it was for the best, that it was what the doctors recommended.'

I shook my head, cheeks wet with tears. 'How could letting me forget Angel ever existed be for the best? She was my identical twin. She deserved so much more than to be cast aside and forgotten because her memory didn't fit with Joyce's stupid pursuit of perfection.'

He reached for me and I stepped back. I couldn't bear it if he touched me. He'd known the truth all these years. He'd watched me suffer, and said nothing. He treated Bill and Joyce as if they really were our parents. I'd counted on him to always be there for me, supporting me, to be the one person I could trust. But it had all been an illusion based on a lifetime of lies.

I spun around and bolted down the hall. Ignoring Daniel's cries for me to stop, I yanked open the front door and ran outside, not caring that I was in my pyjamas and barefoot. I ran down the driveway and onto the empty road, and kept on running, trying to outdistance the pain welling up inside me.

As my feet pounded the bitumen, Angel's image filled my head, the feelings of horror inspired by the dreams magnified tenfold now I knew it was a memory. She had died in the most horrible way, alone and terrified.

A cramp ripped into my side and I stumbled to the side of the road and collapsed on my back on the grassy footpath, gasping in oxygen.

I stared up at the clouds in the sky. What kind of person was I, to forget something like that had happened, to not remember leaving Angel to die?

'Are you okay?'

I shielded my eyes with one hand and stared up at the young guy leaning over me, concern in his rich brown eyes. I swallowed the lump in my throat and gave a nod, not trusting my voice.

'Are you sure? You don't look okay.' He crouched beside me. 'In fact, you look terrible. Your pyjamas are cute though.' He smiled, a dimple appearing in each cheek.

My face heated up as I pushed myself up on one elbow, waving him away when he moved to help. I dragged myself to my feet and peered down at him, arms crossed over the print of a kitten hanging upside down from a branch on my pyjama top.

'So, do you always go for a morning run in your pyjamas or is today a special occasion?' He stood up, and I had to crane my neck to meet his eyes. He had to be well over six feet tall. He brushed dark-brown hair out of his eyes and frowned at me.

'Earth to Andie.'

Eyes wide, I took a step back. 'How do you know my name?' I edged sideways, ready to bolt. I scanned the street, biting my bottom lip when I didn't spot anyone else.

'I met you a couple of months ago, when Dan picked you up from a party for some girl you go to university with. Not surprised you don't remember me, though. You were pretty out of it that night.' His dimples reappeared when he chuckled at the memory.

I tilted my head, thinking back to when I'd attended Maddie's eighteenth birthday party. I'd just started weaning myself off the pills and the dreams had begun once more. Desperate to silence them, I'd made the mistake of thinking alcohol might help me sleep dream-free.

Three drinks later, head reeling, I'd called Daniel and asked him to come and get me. Once he'd got me home I'd slept for twelve hours, unable to wake each time the dream reset. I hadn't touched a drop of alcohol since and cringed to think of this guy seeing me when I'd been so out of it. I hadn't even realised someone else was in the car with Daniel until the other person had helped him get me into the flat.

'So,' he said, 'are you going to tell me what has you running down the road, with no shoes on, or do I have to guess?'

'What are you doing here?' I frowned at him, every muscle in my body tense.

'We had a work function last night and Dan was drinking more than usual. It seemed he had something heavy on his mind, so I thought I'd check on him. I was just pulling up in front of your place when you came flying out the door and tore off down the road.' He tilted his head. 'Want to talk about it?'

I dropped my eyes, the weight constricting my chest increasing. No way was I going to talk about what I'd just discovered to a stranger. He might be Daniel's friend, but he was nothing to me. And seriously, since when did Daniel like being called Dan? He hated it when people shortened his name, or at least he used to.

Maybe I didn't know him as well as I'd thought.

He'd kept the truth about Angel from me, so maybe I didn't know him at all.

4

I turned around to walk home and bit back a curse when my heel came down on something sharp. Balancing on one leg, I lifted my injured foot in the air and groaned when I spotted the bottle top clinging to my heel. It had been partially buried beneath a clump of leaves. I pulled it off, hoping it hadn't punctured the skin. Blood welled from a circular cut and I winced at the sting that erupted now it had been exposed to the air.

Fist clenched around the bottle top, so I could put it in the bin when I got home, saving anyone else from standing on it, I gingerly placed my injured foot on the ground.

'I'll give you a lift. My car's right over there,' said Daniel's friend, getting in front of me and pointing to the dark blue sedan parked across the road.

Eyebrows raised, I stared at him. 'I'm not getting in a car with you. I don't even know your name.'

'Oh, sorry. I'm Nick, Nick Foster.' He held out his hands, palms facing up, and gave me a disarming smile. 'I swear I'm not an axe murderer. And technically, Dan did introduce me the night we brought you home from the party. You just don't remember.'

I took a step back. 'Look, Nick, no offence, but while you might be a friend of my brother's I don't know you, introduction or not. So, you can just go, please. Daniel's fine, I'm fine, and there's nothing for you to worry about.'

Nick let his hands drop, though his smile didn't waver. 'No problem. I'll get out of your way, but at least let me take you home first. No telling what you'll step on between here and there, or how many germs you'll pick up.'

The heel of my foot still stung and, if I were to walk home, I'd have to keep it off the ground the whole way.

Wishing Nick wasn't right about how many germs I could pick up with an open wound, I gave a sigh. 'Fine, you can give me a lift.' Keeping my weight off my heel, I limped across the road and waited while Nick unlocked the car.

He scooted past me to open the passenger door, giving me an engaging grin I did my best to ignore as I slid inside and buckled up. He was just giving me a lift, and I was not in the mood to make a new friend, so I avoided his attempts to start a conversation when he climbed into the driver's seat. He kept shooting sideways glances my way as he drove me back to the flat, and I bolted out of the car as soon as he pulled up out the front.

In my rush to avoid an awkward situation, I put my sore heel on the ground and hissed at the flare of pain. I stumbled back against the car. Before I could regain my balance, Nick had joined me at the kerb, gripping my elbow to steady me. I pulled free of his grasp, but before I could thank him for the ride and ask him to leave, Daniel burst out of the flat.

'Thank God you're back,' Daniel said as he enveloped me in his arms, hugging me tight. 'Don't ever run off on me like that again.'

I held myself still, conscious of Nick watching us. Daniel let me go and stepped back, frowning when he saw his friend.

'Nick? What are you doing here?' He looked from me to Nick. 'What's going on with you two?'

'Nothing is going on with us. He just gave me a lift home.' I brushed past Daniel, back straight, trying to minimise my limp. I walked up the driveway as quickly as I could, my pace not fast enough for my liking, conscious of both of them watching on.

'I was coming to see how you were doing. Found your

sister running down the street with no shoes on,' I heard Nick say. 'Thought I'd better bring her home.'

'Thanks, mate.' Relief coloured Daniel's words.

'Is everything okay? Your sister seemed pretty upset, and you don't look crash hot either,' said Nick. 'Is there anything I can do to help?'

I'd finally reached the front door and didn't wait to hear Daniel's reply. Once inside the flat I headed to the bathroom to get the first aid kit out again. No longer worrying about hiding my limp, I made my way to the lounge room and sat on the couch. I twisted my leg around to inspect the damage I'd done to my heel, not looking up when Daniel walked in.

I stiffened when I realised he wasn't alone. Nick was at his side, the two of them conversing in low tones on the other side of the lounge.

Nick cast a quick glance my way and then crossed the room to take a seat beside me. 'Here, let me do that,' he said as he took the antiseptic cloth out of my hands. 'You're all twisted around like a pretzel.'

My eyes widened as he wiped the cloth over the cut, long fingers gentle and his touch light. He picked up the dressing I had laid out on the seat between us, peeled off the backing and placed the dressing over my heel, smoothing it down and giving me a smile.

'That should do it,' he said, his hand, warm and solid, still resting on my ankle.

I dropped my eyes and pulled my foot free as Daniel stepped closer to the couch.

'Is she going to be okay?' Daniel asked, worry lines appearing on his forehead as he looked to Nick.

'She'll be fine. The cut looked clean.' Nick smiled over at me.

'Hey, I'm right here. I can answer for myself.' I scowled at him. 'And I didn't need your help. I was doing fine on my own.'

'Of course you were, and I'm sorry for taking over like that,' he said, with an apologetic dip of his head. 'I'm the first aid officer for our section at work. I've had to patch up so many scrapes lately, it was an automatic response.'

I stood up, not ready to be appeased by the sheepish grin he wore or the caring light in his dark eyes. So much had happened in such a short time and I needed to be alone to process it, to figure out where to go from here.

'I'm going to get dressed,' I tossed over my shoulder as I limped down the hall.

It was a relief to be able to close my bedroom door, and shut Daniel and Nick out, mind racing as I came up with a plan.

I made my bed and then dressed in jeans and a T-shirt. I hunted in the bottom of my wardrobe for my most comfortable pair of shoes, relieved when I put them on to find they did not press on my sore heel. Next, I headed to the bathroom to wash my face and brush my teeth, conscious of the steady murmur of voices coming from the lounge room.

Nick was still in the flat.

I twisted my hair into a loop and knotted it at the back of my neck, frowning at my reflection the entire time. Why wouldn't he leave?

I needed Daniel to take me to the cemetery, so he could show me where Angel was buried. I also wanted to visit our parents' graves. It had been years since I'd been to the cemetery. I could only vaguely remember going there on a couple of occasions with Bill and Joyce at my back, controlling where I went. No doubt they'd been trying to stop me from spotting Angel's grave.

But that was going to change. Daniel would take me to see Angel, so I could say goodbye.

Maybe then the dreams would stop for good.

My breath hitched when I entered the lounge. Nick stood in the middle of the room, a sympathetic look in his eyes. Daniel was nowhere in sight, though I could hear him talking to someone.

'Dan's outside, on the phone to your parents,' said Nick.

Anger filled me, and I crossed my arms in front of my chest. 'Bill and Joyce are not my parents. They're my aunt and uncle.'

'I thought they adopted you?'

'It takes more than a piece of paper to be parents.'

'I can't blame you for being pissed off with them,' he said, shaking his head. 'Pretty sure I'd feel the same if I suddenly discovered I had an identical twin my folks had never told me about.'

A cold sweat swept over me, mouth hanging open. 'Daniel told you about Angel?'

Nick shrugged. 'He needed someone to talk to. I know you're angry with him, but maybe you can cut him some slack. He's having a hard time dealing with it himself. Still thinks it's his fault your sister died.'

Daniel walked into the lounge, phone in his hand. 'Mum and Dad want to talk to you,' he said, holding the phone out, expression hopeful.

I took the phone, hit the End Call button, and threw it on the floor. 'They can go to Hell, and so can you. I can't believe you told Nick about Angel. It took you fifteen years to tell me the truth, and only then because I found the photo of us as kids. You've known him for what, five minutes, and you tell him everything? How could you do that?'

Daniel didn't even look at me as he scooped his phone off the floor and inspected it for damage.

Teeth gritted, I held out my hand. 'Give me your car keys.'

Daniel straightened up, eyebrows raised. 'What?'

27

'I'm going to the cemetery, so give me your keys.'

'No way. You're not driving my car. You just broke my phone.' He held it up to display a cracked screen, nostrils flaring.

'I don't care about your stupid phone. I just want to see Angel, to say goodbye properly.' Tears pricked my eyes. 'You got to remember her, mourn her, but I never did. Please, Daniel, I need to do this.'

The anger left Daniel's face, and he rubbed a hand over his chin. 'I'll drive you.'

Nick stepped up beside Daniel, putting a hand on his arm. 'Not a good idea, Dan. You had a shitload of drinks last night. You'll still be over the limit. I'll drive you both to the cemetery.'

I glared at him. 'I can drive myself. I don't need either of you to come with me.'

'You are not going to the cemetery alone, and we can't take my car. It's been playing up. I've got it booked in to the mechanic,' said Daniel as he checked his watch. 'Shit, I'm supposed to have it there in fifteen minutes.' He rubbed his chin again. 'Nick, can you follow Andie and me to the mechanic, and then take us to the cemetery?'

'No problem,' said Nick.

There was no way I wanted this virtual stranger coming along on what was going to be an emotional event, but there didn't seem to be another choice. I did my best to ignore him as I waited for Daniel to get dressed and clean himself up, tapping my feet all the while.

'Finally,' I said as Daniel emerged from the bathroom with his face and hair still wet. I stuffed my mobile phone into my back pocket, snatched the keys out of his hand and marched out of the flat, leaving it to him to lock up.

Neither Daniel or I spoke in the car on the way to the mechanic's, yet words hovered in the air around us. As I drove, I sneaked glances his way but, with his sunglasses blocking his eyes, I couldn't tell what he was thinking. My own thoughts were a tangled mess. Guilt over forgetting about Angel warred with anger at being lied to.

Nick's plea for me to cut Daniel some slack was also sinking in, filling me with guilt over how I'd been treating him since I'd confronted him with the truth.

He'd only been seven when the fire had ripped through our home and destroyed our family. Then he'd been manipulated by Bill and Joyce into lying about it. They'd told him keeping the truth from me was for the best, that the doctors had advised it. A seven-year-old wouldn't have known how wrong this kind of reasoning was, and after fifteen years of living the lie it had become a way of life for him.

Maybe the truth would set him free too.

I pulled into the mechanic's car park and waited with Nick while Daniel went inside to hand over the keys and fill out the paperwork. Minutes later, I sat in the back seat of Nick's car, behind Daniel, staring out the window as I steeled myself for coming face to face with my past.

I'd faced Angel night after for night for fifteen years, the memory of what happened to her shrouded in dreams and nightmares.

But this, this was real.

5

When we reached the cemetery, Daniel led the way through manicured lawns, hundreds of plots evenly spaced over the grounds. Large leafy trees offered protection from the harsh sun, while shrubs with flowers provided splashes of colour amongst the grey headstones. I glanced at them as I walked past, taking in the ornaments, cards and flowers people had used to decorate the graves of their loved ones.

I'd been in such a rush to get here, it had never occurred to me to stop to buy flowers for Angel's grave. Then again, flowers would be a paltry offering to make up for so many years of neglect. I'd have to come back, when I was alone, with something that symbolised the bond between twins. No knick-knack would ever make up for forgetting she existed, but it would be a start.

After winding our way through several rows Daniel stopped in the shade of a large tree and pointed at the nearest plot. 'That's where Mum and Dad are buried, but I'm not sure where Angel is.'

I brushed past him and crouched in front of our parents' simple headstone. All it gave was their names and dates of birth and death. Weeds had sprung up and obscured the bottom of the headstone and I brushed them aside, searching for Angel's name. Instead I found blank stone.

I stood and shaded my eyes as I scanned the headstones nearby, but none of them bore her name. 'Why isn't she buried next to Mum and Dad?'

Daniel shrugged as he came to stand beside me. 'I have no idea. But they should have a record of each burial up at the office.'

We'd passed an office on our way through the cemetery. It was close to the carpark, attached to a small chapel. We trudged back that way, and I was pleased to see the office was open on a Saturday morning. I stepped inside, Nick and Daniel at my back, and smiled at the middle-aged woman sitting behind the counter.

'Can I help you?' The receptionist's smile was subdued but friendly, her voice pitched low.

'Yes, please, we're trying to find where Angela Sherman is buried. She died fifteen years ago.' I gave her the exact date.

'Let me see now.' She adjusted her glasses before tapping away on the keyboard in front of her, frowning as she read whatever scrolled up on the computer screen. 'We don't have anyone by that name listed.'

'You must have. Our parents are here. She has to be here too.' My eyes widened. 'Try Angel.'

She tapped away some more, muttering to herself the entire time. She asked me for Angel's date of birth, and typed it in. I tried not to fidget as the computer program begun the next search.

Finally, she shook her head and gave me a sympathetic smile. 'I'm so sorry, dear, I've tried it with both versions of her name, and just the dates of her birth and death in case they misspelled something, but only your parents' burial details are coming up. Perhaps your sister was buried in one of the other cemeteries.'

I shook my head. 'Why would Mum and Dad be here, and not Angel? It doesn't make sense.'

The woman had no answers, so we left the office and stood in the exposed wing of the chapel.

'Angel must be here. She has to be,' I said, looking over the sprawling grounds, searching for a sign, something that

31

would point me in the right direction.

Nick ran a hand through his hair. 'There could have been a glitch in the computer program, I guess, deleting her record. Why don't we split up and check all the graves, see if we can find her that way?'

Relieved to have a reasonable explanation and a plan, I nodded and immediately set off, careful not to put my full weight on my sore heel as I scanned the graves on either side of me. When I reached the end of the row, I made my way to the next one along and walked back the way I'd come. Three rows later I reached the one where Mum and Dad were buried.

A light breeze tickled the back of my neck, and I heard my name whispered on the wind. I lifted my head and searched for Daniel and Nick. They were on opposite sides of the cemetery, still looking at graves, too far away for me to have heard them.

If neither of them had said my name, where had it come from?

I scanned the grounds, spotting a groundsman pushing a wheelbarrow some distance away, but there was no other sign of life.

'Andie.'

I spun around and stared at the vision standing in front of the nearest tree. Angel looked exactly as she had in my last dream, long hair flowing free, white nightgown billowing around her bare feet, a golden glow behind her.

'Angel.' I took a step toward her.

Her form wavered as she held out her hand and pointed south, away from the cemetery. 'Please hurry, Andie. Find me.'

'Where are you?'

Angel kept pointing south as her form grew even more indistinct, and I could make out the shape of the tree trunk behind her. She whispered something else, so faint I couldn't make out the words, before vanishing. I blinked back tears, hand going to my mouth.

Was it real? Had I just seen Angel, or was this a hallucination?

I'd never really thought about ghosts, whether they existed or not, but if they were real, a cemetery would be the most logical place to encounter one. Either that or I really was going crazy.

'Talking to yourself is the first sign of madness, you know.'

I yelped, hands thumping against my chest. Heart racing, I turned around and glared at Nick. 'You scared the hell out of me.'

He gave me a sheepish smile. 'Sorry.'

'And I'm not going crazy. I'm not.' I balled my hands into fists and glared at him.

'Hey, relax, it was just a joke,' he said, an easy grin curving his full lips. 'I don't really think you're crazy.'

I forced my tense muscles to unwind, conscious of the ache from clenching my jaw. I avoided Nick's eyes as I stared in the direction Angel had pointed. How was I supposed to find her, and help her, if she was a ghost? My brain was racing in circles, and I had no idea what to do next.

Shoulders slumped, I shook my head, sure I was going to fail her again.

'Hey, we'll find her. We'll find Angel.' Nick placed a hand on my shoulder and turned me around to face him. 'Don't give up yet.'

I gazed at him, at his earnest brown eyes, the warmth of his hand chasing away the chill that had settled in the pit of my stomach. My fringe fell over my eyes but before I could do anything about it Nick brought up his other hand and brushed it aside, tucking it behind my ear. My skin tingled where he had touched it and I sucked in a breath, confused by the urge to move closer to him.

'Get your hands off my sister.'

Eyes wide, I stepped back when Nick swiftly released me.

Daniel stormed up to his friend and gave his shoulder a not-so-friendly shove. 'Not cool, man. Not cool.'

Nick backed away, hands up and a startled look in his eyes. 'Dan, mate, you've got it wrong. She was upset. I was just trying to make her feel better. I wasn't hitting on her.'

'Damn right you're not hitting on her. She's off limits. Got it?'

I avoided looking at Nick as I confronted Daniel, hands on my hips. 'I am not a child. I can do what I want with who I want, so cut out the over-the-top big brother routine.'

Daniel's eyes narrowed. 'Are you saying you want him to hit on you?'

'What? No.' Heat rose in my cheeks as I willed my voice not to squeak on my denial. 'Of course not. I'm just telling you, for future reference. You don't get to tell me what to do.'

I took off through the cemetery, hoping it didn't look as though I was running away as I headed for the carpark. Now would be a really great time for the ground to open up and swallow me, to save me from ever having to face Nick. He'd just tried to make me feel better and been warned off by Daniel. Then I'd had to go and make it worse. I'd spoken without thinking and made it look as if I was interested in him and that was so not the case.

No way. Not happening.

I'd be an idiot to get involved with my brother's best friend.

'Where are you going? We haven't finished searching.' Daniel caught up and paced along beside me.

'Angel isn't here.'

'You don't know that.'

'Yes, I do.'

'How?'

I stopped walking, struggling to find a way to back up my conviction that didn't involve admitting I'd seen Angel's ghost and been shown the way. A history of nightmares based on a true event was one thing, being able to see and talk to my dead twin was another matter entirely.

I faced Daniel, still careful not to make eye contact with Nick as he stood beside my brother. 'Bill and Joyce have spent the last fifteen years doing everything they could to stop me from remembering Angel. They wouldn't risk me stumbling across her grave and putting it together.'

My explanation started as a way to convince Daniel without having to use the truth, but the more I thought about it the more it made sense. 'There's no record of Angel being buried here because they didn't want her anywhere near Mum and Dad. She's buried in one of the cemeteries on the other side of town, I guarantee it.'

'You make them sound like the villains from a movie. They're not like that.' Daniel shook his head, a frown creasing his brow.

'Says the guy who wasn't drugged for almost his entire life for no reason.' I gave an angry shudder. 'Why can't you see them for who they really are? They are not good people.'

Daniel opened his mouth to protest, but I put up a hand to stop him. 'If they really are as wonderful as you think, then let's go see them. We'll ask them where Angel is buried. If they really care about me then they'll tell me, right?'

I knew it wouldn't be that easy, nothing ever was when it came to my relationship with my adoptive parents. But maybe with Daniel, the favoured one, at my side they would tell the truth for once. I needed more than Angel's simple directions to lead me to her final resting place. If Bill and Joyce did come clean it would save me hours. For a mid-sized town,

Easton had almost a dozen cemeteries. It would take forever to search them all.

'Fine. Let's go see Mum and Dad.'

I narrowed my eyes but let him get away with calling them Mum and Dad, for now. I followed Daniel and Nick back to the car, and climbed into the backseat, going over the dream I'd had of Angel's ghost earlier that morning, trying to remember if there had been anything in it that would help me find where she was buried. Picturing it in my head, all I could see was the electric fence, the trees, and the look of fear on Angel's face.

I stared out the window for the remainder of the drive to the house I'd grown up in. I hadn't been back since I'd moved out and my stomach clenched when Nick pulled into the drive. As I climbed out of the car, I wiped my hands on my jeans and stared at Bill and Joyce's multi-storeyed house.

It had never been a home, not for me. I'd felt more like a guest, often an intruder, forced to inhabit the same space as two people who made clear I was not what they had signed on for. It had been almost unbearable after Daniel had moved out, Bill and Joyce speaking to me only when it was necessary. On some days the only time I even saw them was the nightly ritual where Joyce came to my room with my medication, Bill looming just outside the door, ready to hold me down if necessary.

With a deep breath, I squared my shoulders and walked toward the house, determined this would be the last time I would have anything to do with the people who had stolen so much of my life from me.

6

The front door opened before I reached it and Joyce stepped outside with a wide smile on her face. 'Daniel.' She brushed by me and rushed to hug him.

He hugged her back, though his smile was strained when he finally stepped back and looked over at me. He was just as nervous about this confrontation as I was, perhaps more so. But I wasn't sure if that was because he was anxious on my behalf or hers.

Joyce cast a sideways glance my way, before she eyed Nick. 'And who is this young man?'

'Hi, I'm Nick Foster. I work with Dan.' He held out his hand.

'I see,' said Joyce, ignoring his outstretched hand. 'It is nice to finally meet one of Daniel's work friends,' she said, stressing his full name.

She finally turned to look at me properly, eyebrows raised, and lips pursed. 'Andrea, you know I don't approve of young ladies wearing jeans out in public.' She smoothed down the skirt of her cream sheath dress.

'They're comfortable,' I said with a tight smile.

'Perhaps, but they are hardly ladylike. Why don't you go up to your old room and get changed into something more suitable for entertaining company? You could also do something about your hair, while you're there.' She tapped her sleek chignon with one hand. 'We wouldn't want young Nicholas here to think we didn't raise you right.'

'My hair is fine,' I said, keeping my tone light despite the urge to snap at her. That's what she wanted, but I would not rise to her bait no matter how many digs she threw my way.

'Anyway, I'm sure Nick can handle seeing me in jeans. Right?' I faced him for the first time since the awkward scene at the cemetery, begging him with my eyes to back me up.

Nick grinned as he looked me up and down. 'I'm totally fine with it. I think Andie looks great in jeans. I like her hair just the way it is, too.'

His response earned him a glare from Daniel and a scowl from Joyce, while my cheeks burned at his endorsement. But I toughed it out and faced Joyce.

'See, there's no need for me to get changed.' No way was I ever going to change into one of the dresses or skirts Joyce had insisted I wear while I lived here. I'd left half my wardrobe behind on purpose, my disdain of girly outfits fostered by a lifetime of being told I could at least look like a lady even if I couldn't act like one.

I strode into the house, conscious of Joyce's hard stare at my back, and moved over to the small table positioned beside the door to squirt hand sanitiser into my palms. Then I slipped off my shoes and placed them against the wall with the toes pointing out. Favouring my left heel, I stepped onto the plastic runner that served as a pathway to the spacious formal lounge area.

Behind me, I heard Joyce directing Nick on how to wash his hands and where to place his shoes, making sure he lined them up neatly beside mine. Daniel, familiar with the routine, needed no prompting to follow suit.

In the cream and gold lounge room, Bill was ensconced in his favourite chair, remote control in one hand as he watched the enormous television that took up half the wall opposite.

When I stood in front of him he dropped the remote in his lap, shock on his face as he scrambled to catch it before it fell to the ground. Joyce's stockinged feet made no sound as she slipped across the plush carpet to stand behind her husband's chair. She plucked the remote off his lap and placed it in the holder that hung on the side of his chair, straightening it.

Bill sat up straight and frowned at me. 'Andrea, what are you doing here?'

I leaned forward, purposefully looming over him, so I could catch every expression that crossed his fleshy face. 'Where did you hide Angel?'

He recoiled, the colour fleeing his face. He licked his lips, sweat beading on his brow. 'Wha … what do you mean?' He scrambled out of his seat and moved to stand beside Joyce.

Eyes narrowed, hands on hips, I glared at them both. 'I want to see her. Where did you bury her? We went to the cemetery where Mum and Dad are buried, but they said she's not there.'

Joyce stiffened as she looked at Daniel. 'We?'

He shrugged. 'Andie insisted we go, and I don't blame her. I never got the chance to say goodbye to Angel either, and I'd like to.'

Joyce's expression softened. 'Oh, Daniel. I wish it were that simple.'

'It is,' I said. 'You tell us where she is, and we go see her. Simple.'

'I'm afraid that won't be possible.' Joyce gave a slight grimace. 'You see, the fire was so strong, it took hours before the firefighters could get it under control. By then, there was nothing left of the back of the house where your bedroom was. Your sister's remains were completely destroyed.'

Head swimming, a tight band encircling my chest, I stumbled sideways and sank onto the couch, incapable of taking a breath as the meaning of Joyce's words sank in. The couch dipped as someone sat beside me. They placed an arm around my shoulders, but I didn't look to see who held me, unable to take my eyes off Joyce.

I shook my head. 'That can't be. If Mum and Dad's …

remains were able to be buried, hers would have been too.'

A cruel light gleamed in Joyce's eyes. 'Your parents were on the other side of the house and the coroner's report stated they died of smoke inhalation, whereas your room was completely engulfed in flames. Your sister was a small child. It wouldn't have taken long for the fire to consume her body.'

The arm holding me tightened, drawing me closer, and I sank into the offered embrace. I closed my eyes and burrowed in as I sought to block out the image Joyce's words had prompted. A warm hand stroked my hair as Nick's voice murmured softly in my ear.

'Shush, it's okay. It will be okay,' he said over and over again.

'Did you have to say it like that?' Daniel's voice carried a hint of surprise and rebuke. 'Angel was my sister too. I'm the one that didn't save …' His voice cracked.

'My dear boy, I didn't mean to upset you. I spoke without thinking.'

I opened my eyes and watched as Joyce hurried to Daniel's side and hugged him, genuine remorse on her face. It had been me her comments were intended to wound. I pushed against Nick's chest and he loosened his grip, although he kept his arm around me.

'I don't believe you. Angel's body was not destroyed in the fire. She's somewhere to the south of here, and you're going to tell me where.' I narrowed my eyes, watching as Joyce recoiled.

'That's ridiculous. How could you possibly know that?' Her voice shook, uncertainty clouding her gaze as she looked over at Bill.

I lifted my chin. 'I just do, and I'll search every cemetery in town if I have to, to find her.'

The uncertainty left Joyce's eyes and she gave a smirk. 'It won't do you any good. I'm afraid your sister is long gone.

There's nothing left for you to find.'

The memory of Angel's face, the fear in her eyes as she'd begged me to find her came rushing back. She was out there somewhere, counting on me, and this time I would not let her down. The panicked look Joyce had given Bill when I'd said she was somewhere in the south told me all I needed to know.

I pulled myself out of Nick's arms and stood up, eyes narrowed as I confronted Joyce. 'You're lying. You know exactly where Angel is, and I'm not leaving until you tell me the truth.' I lunged forward, startling her into taking a step back.

'Andie, settle down.' Daniel stepped between us, mouth downturned, facing me. 'I wanted to visit Angel's grave too, but Mum told you what happened. We'll find another way to say goodbye to her, have a memorial service or something.'

I rounded on Daniel, scrambling for a way to get him to see what was right in front of him. 'I'm telling you, she's lying. Angel is on the other side of town.'

'How can you be so sure?'

'Because she told me.'

The second I uttered the words I knew I'd made a mistake.

Joyce moved out from behind Daniel and sneered at me. 'You haven't been taking your medication, have you, Andrea? You're seeing things again.'

'Andie, is that true?' Daniel peered into my eyes, expression wary.

Despite my best intentions, my face gave me away. He moved closer to Joyce, and in that instant, I knew I had lost any chance of his support. But I still fought to make him believe me.

'I wasn't taking tablets because I saw things. It was to stop the recurring nightmares about the fire.'

'That's not exactly true.' The cruel smile was back on

Joyce's face. 'When you first came to stay with Bill and me you claimed you could see your sister, talk to her. That was the main reason we took you to the first psychiatrist. Once you were properly medicated you stopped mentioning your sister and we were encouraged to let you forget her. To say that you have seen her recently, well then it is obvious your decision to stop taking your medication has made you delusional once again.'

Fists clenched, I glared at her. 'I am not crazy, and I know what I saw.'

'So, you did see your sister.' Triumph in her eyes, Joyce pressed home her point. 'I think it would be best if we made an appointment for you to see a psychiatrist as soon as possible. In the meantime, I still have some of your medication. I'll go get it, shall I?'

I shook my head, backing away. 'I am not taking anything.'

Joyce gave a bitter laugh as she advanced on me. 'I'm afraid you don't have a choice. Or would you rather I called the hospital and asked them to place you in their mental health ward until you can be assessed? For your own good, of course.'

7

The vicious light in Joyce's eyes left me in no doubt she would carry through on her threat to have me committed. She didn't so much as blink as she snapped her fingers behind her, urging Bill to grab hold of me.

Panic froze my lungs, making it impossible to suck in air at the thought of being locked up, drugged against my will. I'd rather die than let that happen. I had to get away. I dodged Bill's outstretched arms and ran into the front foyer, careful not to put any weight on my sore heel as I scooped up my shoes and bolted outside.

Behind me everyone started shouting, the sound of Daniel's voice finally breaking the freeze around my lungs. I sucked in air, tears streaming down my face as I ignored his anguished cry for me to stop.

It wasn't until I reached the driveway that I realised Nick was right behind me.

'Get in,' he said as he unlocked his car and opened the passenger door.

I didn't hesitate, climbing inside, slamming the door shut and locking it. Then I twisted around to make sure the back door was locked as well. Entire body shaking, I settled into the seat, wiping away my tears as Daniel ran to the car and banged on the window, calling for me to open up.

Nick climbed into the driver's seat, closed his door and got the car started even as he struggled into his seat belt.

I did up my seat belt as he reversed out of the driveway, Daniel running alongside the car. Nick then changed gears and took off down the street while I craned my head around to watch as Daniel stopped running and stared after us, arms hanging at his sides, features wreathed in grief and worry.

We turned the corner and I lost sight of Daniel. I straightened up and gazed at Nick. He was hunched over the steering wheel, shooting quick glances in the rear-view mirror. When it was clear we weren't being followed, he heaved a sigh and relaxed back in his seat, giving me a sideways grin.

'That was exciting.'

Terrifying.

Soul destroying.

That was what it had felt like to have Daniel turn against me, but I pushed those feelings aside to concentrate on Nick. 'Why are you helping me? Everyone else thinks I'm crazy.'

'From what I just saw, you're the sanest one out of the lot of them. The way she treated you, man, she's a real piece of work.' Nick sent another quick glance my way before returning his attention to the road ahead.

'Besides, I've seen stuff on documentaries about identical twins and the bond they share. Some freaky shit happens to them. There was one I saw, with two women who'd been adopted into different families when they were babies and never knew the other one existed until they were older. When they did find one another, they realised they'd married guys with the same names, had kids around the same time and given them the same names too. Like I said, freaky shit.'

His gaze was thoughtful when he looked over at me again. 'So, are you going to tell me what Angel said to you at the cemetery? That's when her ghost appeared to you, right?'

The tension I'd been holding in flooded out of my body at his ready acceptance, leaving me limp. 'She begged me to find her, and when I asked her where she was she pointed south. That's why I know they're lying about there being no remains to bury. She has to be in one of the cemeteries on the south side.'

'Okay, south it is then.'

We drove in silence to the closest cemetery on the south side. Nick parked directly in front of the office, engine still running, phone in his hand ready to warn me if Daniel or anyone else showed up. Joyce had to know where I'd gone, and I wouldn't put it past her to call the cops to get me arrested or dragged off to the nearest psychiatric ward.

After a quick glance to make sure no one was waiting to leap out at me, I slipped my shoes on and got out of the car to make my way to the office.

'No luck?' Nick asked when I returned to the car fifteen minutes later.

I shook my head, not wanting to talk, a knot forming in my stomach as I remembered how confident Joyce had been that I wouldn't be able to find Angel's final resting place.

After we drove away from the third cemetery I could no longer ignore the fear churning inside me.

'I've tried every version of her name I can think of, and got them to check for burials just using her date of birth and death, but she's not coming up in any of their systems. I'm never going to find her.' Tears stung my eyes and I let them fall.

Nick pulled over and cut the engine. Then he leaned over the centre console to wipe my tears away. 'We've still got a few more cemeteries to go, and the crematorium. Don't give up yet.'

'You were there. You saw Joyce's face the same as I did. She knew I would never be able to find Angel on my own because they made sure she was buried somewhere she couldn't be found.'

Nick rubbed his chin. 'Where do you think they put her?'

I stifled a groan. 'If I knew that we'd already be there.'

Silence filled the car for a time before Nick turned to me

with a hopeful smile. 'Why don't you ask Angel's ghost where they stashed her? She appeared to you before, so get her to do to it again. Only this time ask her to tell you exactly where she is.'

I shook my head. 'Today was the first time she appeared to me outside of my dreams. I have no control over when she contacts me and no idea how to reach out to her.'

'It's worth a try though, right?' He took hold of my hand and stared deep into my eyes. 'Just close your eyes and think about the last time you saw her. See if anything happens.' His dark eyes were intent on mine as he waited for me to follow his suggestion.

I closed my eyes, cheeks heating up. He was so close, leaning toward me, still holding my hand. It was hard to concentrate on anything else when I could hear his even breathing, feel a slight puff of air on my face every time he exhaled.

'Are you sensing anything?'

The heat in my cheeks getting worse, I shook my head and opened my eyes, careful not to meet Nick's gaze. I tugged my hand out of his and moved so my back was against the door, needing more space between us.

'Could you not watch me, please? You're making me nervous.'

'Oh, sorry,' he said. 'I'll just sit here and stare out the window.' He twisted his body around and when I risked a peek he was indeed staring out the window.

I wriggled until I was as comfortable as possible in the confines of the car and closed my eyes again, determined not to think about Nick. Instead I focused on Angel as I had last seen her, long hair flowing free, white nightgown billowing in the wind and fear in her eyes as she begged me to find her.

I drew in a shaky breath as the image of her crystalized in my head, taking me back to the moment in the cemetery when she first spoke to me. The image shifted, distorting, and when my vision of her cleared she no longer stood in front of a tree.

A shiver swept over me at the sight of Angel, strapped down on a bed, electrodes attached to her temples. Long cords connected her to a large machine that sat on a trolley beside the bed. A needle flitted across a ream of paper that fed through the machine, and as I watched the spikes on it grew higher and higher.

Angel moved her head and looked right at me, a warning in her eyes, as a dark-haired woman in a long white coat appeared and pressed a syringe against her arm. A light flared in my head, blinding me. I cried out, rubbing at my closed eyes.

'Andie. What is it? What did you see?'

Eyes watering, I blinked and tried to focus on Nick's face, the nimbus from the light blocking out his features. He cupped my cheeks with both hands. 'Talk to me, Andie. Are you okay?'

I blinked again and again, eyes still smarting, relieved my vision was slowly returning to normal. I attempted a smile when I could finally see Nick's face, wanting to let him know I was okay. He'd gone pale, eyes locked onto mine.

'I'm okay,' I finally managed to say.

Nick let out a sigh, and leaned forward so his forehead rested against mine. 'Don't ever scare me like that again. I thought you weren't going to come back.'

'Come back? I was in the car the whole time.' I pulled away and searched his eyes, surprised to see his hands shaking when he let go of my face.

'Your body may have been, but the rest of you was somewhere else.' He shook his head and ran a hand through his hair. He sank back into his seat, shoulders slumped. 'You just collapsed, went totally limp. I was shaking you for ages, calling your name, but you didn't respond. Scared the hell out of me.'

My gaze fell on the clock in the dash. At least half an hour had passed since he'd suggested I try to contact Angel. Thirty minutes in which I'd been trapped within my vision. Heartbeat accelerating, I struggled to make sense of what I'd seen.

'You saw Angel, didn't you?' Nick asked, reaching out to take my hand again. 'Did she tell you where she's buried?'

For a long moment I said nothing, staring at our joined hands. Finally, I lifted my eyes and met his concerned gaze. 'Angel isn't buried in one of Easton's cemeteries.'

He squeezed my hand. 'You don't believe your aunt, do you, that there were no remains?'

I took a deep breath; sure Nick would think I was crazy and I'd lose my only ally. But there was only one answer that explained my vision.

'I don't think she's dead.' Before he could tell me I was nuts, I launched into a description of what I had seen, closing my eyes to make it easier to remember the details.

'They have to be hiding her in some kind of hospital. The bed she was strapped to had those sides you can put up and down.' Just like the one Daniel was in when he'd had his appendix removed two years ago. 'Who else but a doctor would be wearing a lab coat and giving Angel an injection? And the machine they had her hooked up to looked like an EEG for monitoring brain waves.'

I cut off the torrent of words spilling out of my mouth in my eagerness to convince Nick, holding my breath as I waited for him to tell me I was crazy. Visions, ghosts, dead sisters who weren't really dead... I wouldn't have believed any of this stuff myself if I wasn't experiencing it firsthand.

'Why would they lie about her being dead if she's been in a hospital all this time?' Nick asked.

'Daniel would never have agreed to keep it a secret if he

knew she was alive.' The events of this morning may have dented my faith in my big brother, but I still couldn't believe he would have kept something like that from me. Bill and Joyce had used his guilt over Angel's faked death to manipulate him into doing what they wanted.

'That makes sense, I guess, and it's not much different to them hiding her existence from you for fifteen years,' said Nick. He shuddered. 'Man, I already thought your aunt was scary, but for her to have your sister stashed away somewhere for fifteen years and tell Dan she was dead, she is certifiably insane.'

'You believe me, that Angel is still alive?' I narrowed my eyes, unable to believe he was that easy to convince, even with my crazy aunt thrown into the mix.

Nick gave me a crooked smile. 'Why wouldn't I believe you?'

'Because it all sounds so crazy. I'm seeing my supposedly dead twin sister, talking to her. You've known me for less than a day, and I've dragged you to cemeteries all over town to try to find where she's buried. Now I tell you I don't think she's dead and you're fine with that. How?'

Nick shrugged, a lock of hair falling over one eye. He brushed it away and said, 'I met you months ago, remember, and Dan talks about you all the time. So, it's not as if you're a total stranger. Besides, I told you before that I've seen heaps of documentaries and TV shows about twins, and no one really knows what the human mind is capable of. If you say Angel's alive, then that's good enough for me.'

His crooked smile reappeared. 'And I have to say, if your aunt is involved then anything is possible.'

I couldn't argue with that as I slumped back in my seat. 'That still doesn't tell us where Angel is, and I have no idea where we go from here.'

'Why don't we go back to where it all started? Where did

you live before you moved in with your scary aunt?'

'I have no idea. I was three years old.'

'I bet Dan knows.' Nick let go of my hand and grabbed his phone off the dash. Before I could protest he had dialled Daniel's number.

Daniel answered almost immediately. I could hear only Nick's side of the conversation but the way he kept wincing and the sideways looks he kept shooting my way painted a vivid picture. Daniel was not happy Nick was helping me and I hated to think this could drive a wedge in their friendship. But if Nick was prepared to tough it out, I was happy to let him.

Nick kept his tone light, despite whatever Daniel was saying to him. 'Come on, Dan. You know Andie's not like that. She just wants to say goodbye to your sister. If your aunt is telling the truth about what happened in the fire, then your old house is the closest place there is to a grave. Cut us some slack and give me the address. I promise I'll bring Andie back home as soon as she's had some time to accept what really happened to Angel.'

Nick held a finger to his lips when I started to protest and I reluctantly subsided, not sure if I liked where his conversation was going, aware of what I would face if he did take me back to Bill and Joyce's house. They'd jump on this as an excuse to get me locked away, out of their hair and out of Daniel's life.

Just as they did to Angel.

Nick finally hung up the phone and gave me a grin. 'No need to look so serious. I've got the address and it's not that far from here. We're good to go.'

My arms were crossed in front of my chest. 'You told him you would take me back to Bill and Joyce's after we go to the old house.'

'Relax, Andie. I said I'd take you back after we found out

what really happened to Angel. Not once did I say I was taking you straight there after we checked the place out.' His grin widened, and I smiled along with him. My smile quickly faded when he started the car again.

'What if we don't find anything? What if we never find out what happened to Angel?'

'Then I guess you're stuck with me forever,' he said, pretending to leer.

I rolled my eyes, my black mood somewhat lifted by his antics. It lifted even more when he took one hand off the wheel and covered mine where it rested on my lap.

'Hey, we'll find her. You just have to stay positive.'

I nodded, and his hand tightened on mine. He didn't let go as he steered the car onto the road. He finally released my hand when we reached an intersection. He navigated through the give way sign, and a pang of disappointment hit me when he didn't reach out and take my hand again once he'd turned the corner. When he was touching me, I felt less alone and it was easier to be positive.

I forced my disappointment down. I couldn't afford to get attached to Nick. No matter how keen he appeared to be to help me find Angel, how willing he was to believe I had a connection with my twin, he was still a stranger. Today had taught me not to rely on my own flesh and blood. Daniel siding with Bill and Joyce, and hiding a monumental secret from me, made it impossible to believe a stranger would prove to be more trustworthy than my own brother.

I was starting to think the only person I could truly count on was me.

To find Angel, save her from whatever it was that woman in the lab coat was doing to her, I had to be strong, for both our sakes.

8

Ten minutes later, Nick pulled up in front of a large two-storey house with landscaped lawns and a shiny red sports car parked in the driveway. The house was beautiful, modern, and from the look of it had been built in the last few years.

Nibbling on my bottom lip, I looked over at Nick. 'You must have got the address wrong. I don't remember anything about our old house, but I'm pretty sure this isn't it.'

He reached over and took my hand, giving it a slight squeeze. 'This is the right address. Dan said your old place was torn down after the fire.'

My stomach sank as I stared at the house, my hope of finding a clue to Angel's whereabouts fading. I shouldn't have been surprised, really. The dreams had shown me over and over how bad the fire had been. But looking at the house now I realised I'd envisioned myself walking down the hall, standing in the room I had once shared with Angel, exorcising the memory that haunted my dreams and replacing it with a new reality. I covered my mouth with my free hand, unable to stifle my sobs.

Nick let go of my other hand and I heard his door open and then close. Seconds later my door opened, and he crouched in front of me. He unbuckled my seatbelt and then drew me out of the car, wrapping me in his arms as I cried into the front of his shirt.

'Hey, it's okay. It will be okay,' he said, his words rumbling through his chest as he rubbed my back.

Clutching his shirt in my hands, I shook my head. 'No, it won't,' I said, my words muffled as I pressed against him.

'There's nothing left. How am I supposed to find Angel with nothing to go on?'

'Hey, I wouldn't have brought you here if I thought it was going to be a dead end.' I could hear the smile in his voice. 'There's got to be someone in this street who lived here back then. We're going to knock on doors and ask if any of them remember anything from that night.'

I shifted so I could see his face, his dimples appearing as he smiled down at me. He looked so optimistic, but I wasn't ready to have my hopes dashed again.

'Fifteen years is a long time,' I said.

'True, but it's worth a shot. All it takes is one person to remember something to give us a place to start.' He gave me a crooked smile. 'Right?'

'Right.' I managed a wobbly breath as I eased myself out of his arms and scanned the rest of the houses in the street. Being a Saturday, there was a high chance we would catch some of the residents at home. A couple of the houses looked to have been renovated over the years, but many more appeared to be the original homes.

The side of the street we were standing on had more of the older style houses. Hoping this was a sign the residents might have been there a while, I said, 'I'll do this side, you do the other.'

Nick nodded, and we walked in silence to the beginning of the street.

'Good luck,' he said, one hand snaking around the back of my neck to pull me closer. Eyes wide, I sucked in a deep breath as he leaned in and gently brushed his lips across mine.

It was the lightest of touches, could barely even be described as a kiss, and yet the feel of his lips on mine filled me with a giddy sense of excitement and a yearning to press my mouth firmly against his. But before I could do anything he released me and then turned and darted across the street.

Frozen in place, unable to take my eyes off Nick as he strode up to the front door of the first house, I ran a finger over my lips, amazed at the sensations still flooding my body from the almost-kiss. The loud rap as he knocked on the door across the street jolted me from my daze. I dropped my hand and turned around to open the gate of my first house.

The front door was closed and after I pressed the doorbell I did my best to tidy myself, sure my outsides reflected the inner turmoil racing through me. A young woman answered the door and I pushed thoughts of Nick aside.

'Hi, my name's Andie and I used to live in this street when I was little. I was hoping to talk to people who lived here fifteen years ago.'

'Sorry,' she said, with an apologetic shrug. 'We've only been here six months.'

'That's okay,' I said, forcing down my disappointment to give her a slight smile. 'Thank you for your time.'

It was too much to expect to get a positive result at the very first house. But there were plenty more to go. One of the residents was sure to have been living here back then. I lifted my head, plastering on a smile as I prepared to knock on the front door of the next house along.

Half an hour later, a dull ache at the back of my head, I knocked on the door of a small cottage. My earlier optimism was deflated by over two dozen failures to discover anyone who had lived here when I did. I doubted the remaining three houses on my side would prove different.

The front door of the cottage was open behind a locked security door, so I knew someone was home though no one appeared in response to my knock. A hallway ran through the middle of the house, and I could see the back door was also open, and blocked with a security door.

'Hello? Is anyone there?' I knocked again and repeated my call. Perhaps I should go around the side of the house, to see if they were in the backyard.

Before I could take a step, I heard a faint voice from somewhere deep inside the house. 'I'm coming. I'm coming. Just give me a minute.'

A moment later, an old man appeared from a room at the end of the hall nearest the back door, leaning heavily on the walking frame in front of him. It was an effort to keep my smile in place and not fidget as he shuffled his way down the hall toward me.

He finally reached the door, fingers fumbling with the glasses hanging on a chain around his neck. He placed them on his nose and peered through the screen, blinking rapidly.

His eyes widened, and he clutched his chest. 'Angel.'

I sucked in a breath. 'You've seen her?' A quiver of excitement surged through me, setting my pulse racing as I leaned forward, hands on the screen. 'Please, I'm trying to find her. Do you know where she is?'

The old man's hand shook as he reached over and unlocked the security door. 'I think you'd better come inside.'

'Thank you, thank you so much. I just need to get my friend. I'll be right back.' Without waiting for a reply, I bolted to the footpath and scanned the street for Nick. He was just coming out of the house directly opposite me and I couldn't contain my smile as I shouted his name and waved him over.

He bounded across the street, his smile just as wide as mine. 'You got something?'

'He called me Angel.' I pointed over my shoulder to where the old man stood in the doorway. 'He's seen her.'

Nick gave a whoop and grabbed me around the middle, swinging me around and around. Breathless, I laughed as I asked him to put me down. He did so, waiting until I was steady on my feet before he let go of my waist. Then he took my hand and together we rushed up the path to where the man held the door open for us.

55

Nerves singing, hoping this was the break through we'd been looking for, I tried to stamp down my impatience as the old man turned his walking frame around and shuffled back down the hall.

He led us into a small lounge room crowded with furniture, stopping once he was halfway in to stare at me, confusion covering his face. 'I'm Pete Simpson, and you look just like Angel. But you're not her.'

'I'm her sister, Andie, and this is Nick.'

'Well, Andie and Nick, I think it's time I sat down.' He grimaced. 'These old legs don't like to do their job for long these days.' He set his walker beside a large armchair and then lowered himself into it with a sigh.

'Sit, sit,' he said, waving his hand at me and Nick. 'Having people standing when I'm sitting makes me uncomfortable; hurts my neck to keep looking up all the time.'

Nick, still holding my hand, tugged me over to one of the two seater couches positioned on either side of Mr Simpson's armchair and pulled me down beside him. I perched on the edge of the seat, body tense, unable to relax when I was so close to finding my sister. He'd called me Angel, recognised me instantly, so he must have seen her recently.

Angel was alive, and I was going to find her.

9

'Mr Simpson, do you know where Angel is?' I held my breath as I waited for him to answer, stomach plummeting when he shook his head.

'But you have seen her,' said Nick, squeezing my hand.

'Yes, I saw her. It was about six months ago, before my son had the security door installed.' He shook his head. 'He'd been on my case about being more careful, but I can't stand to feel as if I'm locked up in my own home, so I always leave the doors open, to let the breeze travel through the house. That day, I was in the kitchen, making myself some lunch, when I heard a noise in the lounge. I came in and saw my lamp had been knocked over.'

He pointed at a lamp sitting on a small table at the end of the couch opposite the one Nick and I were perched on.

'At first, I thought it must have been the wind that knocked it down, but when I went over to straighten it I realised someone was crouched behind the couch. Just about gave me a heart attack. Thought my son had been right all along and I was about to be belted over the head and robbed. Then she stood up.' His eyes gleamed as he smiled at me, unshed tears shimmering in his eyes. 'You look just like her, like an angel come to life. When I saw her, I thought my time had come and she was there to usher me off to Heaven.'

His smile faded, expression now grim. 'Then two men burst into my house, calling for Angel. Didn't surprise me to hear her name fitted her appearance, but it didn't take long to figure out those guys were up to no good.'

Tears glimmered in his yes. 'Your poor sister, she was

terrified. She tried to run, to get past them, but they grabbed her by the arms and dragged her out of here. Her mouth was open, as if she was screaming, but I never heard her make a sound. I tried to go after them, to see if I could help her, but by the time I got to the front door they had her in the back of a white van. They drove off and I never saw her again.'

Anger stiffened my spine, the memory of the vision with Angel strapped to the bed fuelling my rage. Whoever these people were, I would make them pay for hurting my sister.

'These men, do you know who they were, where they came from?' Nick asked.

'I called the police and gave them the licence plate of the van as soon as I got back inside. They promised to look into it, and I got a phone call from them a week later. Longest week of my life, and all he said was that Angel had escaped from a mental institution and those men were orderlies, sent to find her and take her back.'

He shook his head again, mouth twisted up as though he'd tasted something bad. 'The officer I spoke to told me not to worry, that she was being taken care of. But I've never been able to stop thinking about her. She was so frightened, and they weren't being gentle when they dragged her out of here.'

I leaned forward. 'Did the police tell you what institution she was in?'

'No, and believe me, I asked. I wanted to visit her, see for myself if she was all right. But they said she wasn't allowed visitors. That she was in isolation for her own good. I can't see how being kept apart from other people could be good for anyone, let alone a young woman.'

I got up and started to pace, fists clenched at my sides. 'We have to find her. We have to get her out of there.'

Nick stood and stilled my pacing by placing his hands on my shoulders, and then they moved to my neck, his thumbs stroking along either side of my jaw as he made me look at him. 'We will. We'll find her.'

'You're her sister,' said Mr Simpson. 'An identical twin from the looks of it. How come you don't know where she is?'

Legs suddenly weak, all the tension that had led me to this point dissipating in a rush, I fought back tears as I said, 'I didn't even know she existed before this morning, and then I was told she died fifteen years ago. But I knew they lied. I knew she was alive, somewhere. I just didn't know where.' I moved away from Nick and knelt in front of the old man, clasping his hands in mine.

'Thank you for caring about Angel, Mr Simpson, for trying to help her. You're a good person.'

He gave me a rueful smile. 'I don't know about that. It just didn't sit right with me, her being so scared of them and all. When you find her, will you bring her to see me, so I know for sure she's doing okay?'

'Of course I will.' I let go of his hands and got to my feet.

Wiping away my tears with the back of one hand, I walked to the front door and let myself out of the house, with Nick right behind me. Once I reached the footpath I pulled my phone out of my back pocket and opened a search engine.

'There can't be that many mental institutions in town,' I said to Nick as I tapped away on the screen.

Nick got out his phone as well. 'Good idea. I'll check out the online phone directory.'

Eyes on our phones, we walked back toward Nick's car as we discussed the possibilities that came up in our search.

'Looks like the public hospital and all the private ones have Mental Health Units,' I said, 'but in the dream I had this morning, Angel was being chased through a property that was filled with trees. It had a fence that looked to be at least a couple of metres high, and there was a sign saying it was electrified. They wouldn't be able to have something like that in the middle of town. It has to be somewhere more isolated.'

'I found a place called the Wood Estate. It's listed as a Mental Health and Rehabilitation Centre. The write-up on it says they specialise in caring for troubled adolescents. It's a few kilometres out of town, on the highway leading west,' said Nick, angling his phone so I could see the place he was talking about. 'Could be worth a look.'

'Andie.'

I froze at Daniel's shout and looked up from my phone, eyes narrowed when I spotted him standing on the footpath near Nick's car. He was flanked by Bill and Joyce, and my top lip curled back at the sight of the two people I had ample reason to hate most in the world. I shoved my phone back into my pocket and marched up to the three of them, gaze fixed on Joyce.

'What the hell are you doing here?'

'We're here to help you,' said Daniel, reaching out to grab my arm. 'You're sick. You need to go to the hospital.'

I pulled away from him, still not talking my eyes off Joyce, wanting to witness the moment she realised all her lies were about to come crashing down. 'Where I need to go is the Wood Estate. Isn't that right?'

Panic flared in her gaze and she quickly glanced over at Bill, who looked just as concerned. She quickly covered her surprise and gave me a cool smile.

'I don't know what you're talking about, Andrea. We're just trying to help you, but it's clear you're not ready to accept that quite yet.' She reached out to clutch Daniel's arm. 'We can't help your sister until she is ready to accept she has a problem. We would just be wasting our breath, so we might as well go.' She tugged on his arm, trying to lead him toward where her car was parked behind Nick's.

'What?' The look of surprise on Daniel's face at Joyce's words would have been comical if I didn't know what was behind her sudden about-face.

'He's not going anywhere with you,' I said. 'It's time he found out just what a pair of lying, conniving snakes you really are.'

Daniel's eyes were wary when I faced him fully and said, 'Bill and Joyce have been lying to you for fifteen years. Angel isn't dead. She's trapped in a mental institution, and I'm going to get her out. Are you coming?'

Daniel shook his head, taking a quick step back from me. 'Andie, no. You're sick, delusional. You need to come with us, so we can get you back on your medication.'

'I am not delusional. I'm telling the truth. Nick and I just spoke to an old man who saw Angel, in his house, six months ago. She's alive, Daniel. Bill and Joyce lied to you, the same way they lied to me.'

His eyes widened as he tossed his head. 'No, no way. They wouldn't lie about something like that. Not to me.'

His words made me grimace. He had always been the golden child, never having cause to doubt Bill and Joyce's love for him. I was about to destroy a significant part of his identity and, even though it had to be done, I wished I didn't have to be the one to do it.

'Look at them, Daniel. Look at their faces. They would do whatever it took to ensure their version of a perfect life was the only one you ever knew. Angel didn't fit in their world, so they got rid of her and told you she was dead.'

Slowly, mouth downturned, Daniel twisted around and looked to Bill and Joyce, searching their faces for answers. 'Mum, Dad, is it true? Is Angel alive?'

Bill shuffled his feet, head down. 'Don't listen to her, son. She's crazy. You heard her earlier, she said she was seeing things. You can't believe a word she says.' Despite the conviction in his voice, he wouldn't meet Daniel's eyes.

'For goodness sake, Daniel, how could you ask us that?

We're your parents. We wouldn't lie to you about something like this.' Joyce's nostrils flared, red blooming in her cheeks. 'Andrea has always been jealous of our closeness. She's trying to drive a wedge between us. That's all this is.'

'Really? Then how do you explain Mr Simpson finding Angel in his lounge room, and two men dragging her out and throwing her into the back of a van?' Nick glared at Joyce.

'This has nothing to do with you, young man. This is a family matter, so you keep your opinions to yourself.' Bill puffed out his chest.

Nick laughed in his face. 'You're not a family. You and your wife are a pair of parasites who don't deserve to be parents. Andie is an amazing person, and you've done everything you could to ruin her life. But not anymore. She is going to find her sister, and you will lose the best thing that ever happened to you.'

The fierceness of his tone and his readiness to back me up made me smile. Daniel, on the other hand, did not look impressed to witness his friend tearing into our aunt and uncle. I got between them, determined to remove the blinders fifteen years of being in Bill and Joyce's care had afflicted him with.

I needed him.

Angel needed him.

I had to make him believe me.

10

I wanted to shake Daniel, make him see the truth, but that was not the way to do it. Instead I took a steadying breath and begged him to listen. 'I know it's hard for you to believe me after years of being told I'm crazy, but you don't have to take my word for it. We can go see Mr Simpson and he can tell you exactly what happened himself. He said he filed a police report, after he saw Angel. We can even go down to the station, if you want, if that's what it takes to get you to listen to me.'

'Come away from her, Daniel,' said Joyce, voice strident, gesturing for Bill to grab his arm.

Daniel stepped out of reach, hands up to ward Bill off, his head swivelling as he tried to watch all of us at once. Confusion wreathed his features and my heart ached for him. He really believed they loved us both, that I was being too hard on them. I'm sure they did love him, in their twisted way, but any soft feeling they might have had for me had died as soon as my nightmares started.

Joyce glared at me, not making any effort to disguise her true feelings now. 'This nonsense has gone on long enough, Andrea. I'm calling the hospital.' She reached into her handbag. 'They can send someone to come and get you. You need to be locked up, for your own good,' she spat out. 'We should have put you away years ago.'

'Was that why you had Angel locked up? For her own good?' I snatched the phone out of her hand and tossed it on the ground, disappointed when it didn't smash into pieces on impact. 'She didn't fit your idea of the perfect child, because she couldn't talk. That's why you put her in a mental institution, and told Daniel she died in the fire. Tell the truth for once in your miserable life, Joyce. You locked her away, kept her from us, all because you didn't want to have to take care of a mute child. Isn't that right?'

Joyce shoved me backwards, and I would have fallen if Nick hadn't caught me.

Face twisted into a mask of hate, she glared at me. 'Your sister is a freak, just like you turned out to be. I wish both of you had died in the fire with your parents.'

'Mum, no, what are you saying?' Daniel caught her arm, his confusion giving way to dismay.

Joyce stumbled, desperation in her gaze as she reached for Daniel, hands cupping his face. 'Sweetheart, you must understand. There is something seriously wrong with them. They are not normal. Your parents ignored the warning signs, refused to put your other sister in care when she was first diagnosed. Then they died, leaving it to me to clean up their mess and do what they should have done in the first place.'

Daniel pulled out of her grasp and dropped her arm. He stepped back, horror on his face as he looked over at me and then back to her. 'So, it's true. Angel really is alive.'

'Listen to me. We did it for you. Your sister is not right in the head. Bill and I didn't want you to have to suffer the burden of caring for someone like that. You have no idea what it takes to care for a person who is mentally ill. Look at all the trouble we've had with Andrea.'

Daniel shook his head, warding off Joyce's attempts to touch him. 'You lied to me. You let me believe Angel was dead, that it was my fault.'

'It would have been better if she had died,' said Bill. 'Instead she somehow managed to get out through the window in her room. The firemen found her, unconscious in the backyard, after they put the fire out.'

'You'd rather she'd died? What kind of monster are you?' Nick shook his head.

'Keeping her in private care all these years has cost Bill and me a fortune, and now we'll have to pay for Andrea as well.' Joyce spun around and sneered at me. 'You'll finally get to be with your sister, locked up in a mental institution, where you belong.'

'You are not putting Andie in a mental institution.' Daniel pushed past Joyce and made his way to my side, fists clenched.

'I have no choice. She's sick. You heard her this morning. She admitted to seeing your sister, to talking to her, when that's impossible.'

Daniel's voice was flat when he said, 'Her name is Angel, and she's my sister too, a fact you seem to have forgotten.'

'Son, don't take that tone of voice with your mother.' Bill's fleshy face was red, sweat making it glisten, pale eyes fuming. 'I won't have you disrespecting her.'

Daniel's laugh was bitter. 'She's not my mother. Andie's right. It takes more than a piece of paper to make you our parents.' He turned his back on Bill and Joyce and gave me a lopsided smile. 'I'm so sorry for not believing you, for keeping Angel a secret from you for so long. Can you forgive me?'

'Of course I can.' I launched myself into his arms, crying on his shoulder as I hugged him with all my strength, while his arms wrapped around me in an equally tight embrace.

After a long moment, I drew back. 'Let's go get Angel.'

'That is never going to happen,' said Joyce. 'We are her legal guardians and we've made sure she never leaves that place.'

I lifted my chin and faced her. 'Angel is eighteen, legally an adult, so she doesn't need a guardian. Besides, Daniel and I are her family. They will give her to us.'

'No, they won't. But be my guest, go ahead and try to get her released.' She looked down her nose at me, and then shifted her attention to Daniel.

'Daniel, I understand you feel betrayed by us, but in time you will understand we did it to spare you the pain of knowing your sister had survived the fire but had to be institutionalized because of her worsening mental state. She's violent, hurting herself and others, and if Andrea doesn't get treatment soon she'll end up the same way.'

Joyce bent down and scooped her phone off the ground. 'Although, if you're so set on going out to the Wood Estate I'll ring ahead and let them know you're coming. They can have a room ready for Andrea, next to her sister.'

I shook my head. 'You can't even say her name. Angel isn't even a person for you.'

Joyce didn't bother to answer. She took Bill's arm and pulled him toward their car. She had her phone up to her ear and was talking into it, and I had no doubt she was calling the Wood Estate.

'Now what are we going to do?' Nick asked, touching my arm.

I frowned as I gazed at him. 'We're going to go get Angel, of course.'

'What if they try to lock you up, too?'

'I don't think it's that easy to get someone committed,' I said. 'At least, I hope it's not. Either way, I'm not going to let that stop me from finding Angel. She's been trapped in that place for fifteen years, alone, forgotten. I don't want her to spend another day in there.'

'I'm with Andie,' said Daniel. 'We are going to get Angel back today, no matter what it takes.'

'We better get there fast, then, before whatever welcoming committee your crazy aunt is cooking up gets time to plan a way to lock Andie up as well,' said Nick.

66

With the thought of the reception we might receive, we were subdued as we piled into Nick's car. Daniel ushered me into the back seat and then joined me, Nick remaining silent as he drove us to the Wood Estate to give us a measure of privacy. But before Daniel could launch into what would no doubt be a tear-jerking confession or apology from the look on his face, I reached out and took his hand.

'It's okay. You don't need to say it.' I gave him a watery smile. 'You have always been the best brother you could possibly be, and I have never doubted that you love me. We'll get Angel back and somehow we'll make it up to her, together. Everything else is in the past. It's time for us to move on, as a real family this time.'

Some of the darkness in his eyes lifted and he pulled me close, slinging his arm around my shoulder. 'Anyone tell you you're not too bad, for an annoying little sister?'

I grinned back at him, and we sat like that for the rest of the drive, only moving apart when Nick stopped the car at the entrance to the estate. It was situated just off the highway, a large wrought iron gate opening onto what looked like a long and winding driveway. I craned my neck. I couldn't see any buildings from where we were, but there was no doubt we were in the right place.

Two tall, wide brick columns stood on either side of the driveway, the gates hinged from them, each one bearing a plaque with the name the Wood Estate hanging from the top. A two-metre heavy duty mesh fence ran the length of the visible frontage, but there were no danger signs as in my dream, so it didn't appear to be electrified. Not that I planned on touching it to find out.

'Are you guys ready for this?' Nick twisted in his seat to look at us.

Daniel squeezed my shoulder and I gave a nod, peering forward as he got the car moving again. Hundreds of trees lined the driveway, spreading their boughs over the road and creating a natural tunnel.

It was dark, shadowed, making me think the name of the Wood Estate was a reference to the trees surrounding the institution. Not that it gave the place a fairy-tale vibe. It put me more in mind of a haunted forest, a feeling that intensified when we rounded the last bend and I caught my first sight of the institution itself.

It was a wide, ugly building, three storeys high, built from a dark grey stone. An effort had been made to lighten the facade with numerous windows, but as all the ones in the top two floors were covered by thick bars, the effect made it look more like a prison than a place where people came to get better. As Nick drove us closer, I spotted the electric fence from my vision.

It ran from the sides of the building and disappeared into the trees, presumably enclosing the back section of the estate, making it impossible for patients to escape. The only access to the estate itself was through the wide glass doors directly in the centre of the ground floor. This was not a place I imagined many people would be comfortable visiting, let alone being stuck in.

A large turning circle for vehicles was in front of the building, with dozens of car parks set out on either side of it. The carpark to the left had a sign stating it was for staff only, while the right was for visitors. As Nick headed for a park in the relatively empty visitors' section, I surveyed the one on the left and did not like what I saw.

The closest parks in the staff area were taken up by three white vans and two security vehicles, and there had to be at least a dozen other vehicles spread through the area. If these people didn't hand Angel over to us willingly, we were going to be seriously outnumbered. Not that I would let that stop me. I was taking my sister home, no matter what any doctor, security guard or staff member had to say about it.

I climbed out of the car and got ready to march inside and demand they release Angel. Nick cut me off before I could take three steps.

'Let's be smart about this,' he said, his expression more serious than anything I had seen previously, without a dimple in sight. 'If your aunt is to be believed, she's primed these people to lock you up the second you set foot in there. We can't risk you getting trapped as well. Dan and I will go in first, and see what they say. I need you to wait in the car until we know if it's safe for you to come in or not.'

'No. No way.' I crossed my arms in front of me and glared at him. 'My sister is in there, counting on me to free her.'

'I know, I know.' He gave me an apologetic smile. 'I totally understand that you want to be the one to save Angel, but until we know what reception we're going to receive, the smart thing for us to do is keep you in reserve. You're the only one of us that has a chance of contacting Angel if something goes wrong. They get a hold of you, lock you up with Angel, Dan and I are going to have a hard time storming the place to get you out again.'

He dipped his head, his grin firming and the dimples reappearing. 'We'll do it, sure, but why don't we see if we can get this done without them calling the cops on us?'

'We don't even know if Joyce has managed to get her way. Just because she wants them to commit me doesn't mean they'll do it,' I said. 'You could be worrying about nothing.'

'No, Nick's right,' said Daniel. 'We have a much better chance of getting in to see Angel if you stay out here. You're her identical twin. Even if they haven't been warned to keep a look out for you, your appearance could make them suspicious. We can't risk it. You need to stay in the car. Please.'

I didn't like it, but with the two of them looking at me with matching expressions of concern, I knew I had to give in. 'Fine, I'll wait in the car. But I'm telling you right now, we are not leaving this place without Angel.'

11

I tapped my fingers on the dash as I waited in the front passenger seat for Nick and Daniel to return. They'd been gone for quarter of an hour and with every passing minute my stomach knotted even more. Eyes fixed on the front door, I willed them to hurry up and get out of there. The longer it took, the more convinced I was that something had gone wrong.

The urge to jump out of the car and go looking for them was so strong I had to dig my nails into my palms to restrain myself. Seconds away from throwing all caution aside, I stiffened when a shiver swept over my body, sure I could hear Angel calling my name.

I twisted to inspect the back seat, the feel of her presence so clear I expected her to appear in the car. The backseat was empty and there was no sign of her when I scanned the car park. My sense of her faded and I closed my eyes, trying to call her back, to connect with her and let her know we were close to freeing her. But no matter how hard I strained, I couldn't get through. It was as though an impenetrable wall stood between us.

A loud rap on my window made me jump and I snapped my eyes open. A man with greasy blond hair tied back in a ponytail and dressed in a light blue orderly's uniform peered in at me. He was huge, his wide shoulders blocking out the entire window. He sneered at me, dark eyes filled with malice as he tugged on the door handle.

I tensed, ready to kick, punch and bite my way to freedom. But the door didn't open, and I sagged in relief, remembering Nick had used his key remote to lock the doors after I'd got in the front seat.

The orderly's expression darkened, and he wrenched on the handle again and again. Then he took a step back, swinging his body around with his elbow raised. He was going to try to break the window. Heart pounding, I scanned the interior of the car, looking for something, anything, to fight him off with.

But there was nothing I could use.

'Hey, you, get away from her.' Nick appeared beside the orderly and pushed him back, causing him to stumble.

The orderly quickly recovered his footing, snarling as he rushed forward, fists raised, and threw a punch at Nick's head. Nick dodged, and the orderly's fist connected with the side of the car. The orderly howled and clutched his hand as Daniel shot into view. He shoved the orderly to the ground and then launched himself at the back passenger door as Nick pressed the button on his key remote to unlock the car.

Daniel dived into the backseat and Nick sprinted around the front of the car. I leaned over and opened the driver's side door and Nick jumped into the seat. The orderly scrambled to his feet. Nick inserted the key in the ignition and hit the accelerator as the orderly slammed his elbow into my window.

The window held, and Nick put the car in reverse, tyres squealing as he quickly righted the car and took off down the winding driveway, leaving the orderly cursing as he ran after us. I twisted in my seat to see if we were being followed, rapidly losing sight of the estate, body swaying with each turn as the car picked up speed. We shot out onto the highway, with no sign of pursuit.

Tears pricked my eyes and I hurriedly dashed them away. I'd vowed I wouldn't leave the estate without Angel, and had fled at the first sign of trouble. I'd failed her again.

I looked to Daniel, his expression as crushed as mine must be. 'Did you get to see her?'

He grimaced. 'No, we only got to see her doctor, Joanna Wood. She claimed it would set back Angel's treatment if she had visitors. She refused to listen when I said we were taking her out of there.'

'Wood, as in the Wood Estate?' So, it hadn't been named for the trees surrounding it. 'This doctor, is she the one in charge of that place?'

'Yes, and pretty pleased with herself, too,' said Nick, a snort following his words. 'There were over a dozen photos of her on the walls in the reception area. In one of the more recent ones, for some kind of reunion, she's standing beside your scary aunt. They looked pretty chummy, all done up in ball gowns.'

'I guess that explains how they have been able to keep Angel locked away all this time, if the doctor and Joyce are friends,' I said. 'But even if they were the best friends in the world, what kind of doctor would agree to commit Angel when there was nothing wrong with her other than being mute? She would be risking her career, if the truth came out. Surely someone on the staff had to realise Angel didn't belong there. Why didn't any of them do something about it?'

'Dr Wood is the one who signed off on Angel being committed in the first place. Her signature is on the paperwork, along with Bill and Joyce's. It's dated the day after the fire, so they didn't waste any time getting rid of her,' said Daniel, shaking his head in dismay. 'She must have been so scared. First the fire, and then to be put in a place like that.'

'You saw her paperwork?'

He grimaced. 'Dr Wood sent her receptionist to fetch it after I threatened to go to the police. Told me I would be wasting their time if I called them. That once they checked over the paperwork they would realise she had every legal right to keep Angel locked up, and you too.'

'What?' My eyebrows shot up.

'The paperwork is already filled in, with Bill and Joyce's signature and everything. Dr Wood said that as soon as they found you they would be locking you away as well, for your own good.'

I shook my head. 'That's impossible. Bill and Joyce couldn't have signed those forms. They couldn't have beaten us here.'

Daniel reached out and clasped my shoulder. 'The date on the form is from six months ago, the day before you turned eighteen.'

I gasped. 'They were planning on having me committed all along.'

'I guess they knew you'd go off your medication, and were waiting for the right moment to act,' he said with a shrug.

I slumped in my seat, body shaking.

'Hey,' said Nick as he reached over and took my hand. 'We won't let them get you.'

I gave him a watery smile. 'What if she's right? What if that paperwork is legally binding?' If Dr Wood had the law on her side, my chances of freeing Angel were slim at best. Worse, even, if I got locked up with her.

'They can't commit you if they can't find you,' said Nick. 'In the meantime, we can work on getting your sister out of there.'

'You can't go home,' said Daniel. 'That's the first place they'll look for you.'

'She can stay at my place,' said Nick.

Daniel frowned. 'You live in a two-bedroom flat, same as we do, with another guy. Where would she sleep?'

Nick shrugged. 'Matt is on shift at the mine for the next eight days. She can stay in his room. No problem.'

'Are you sure?' I asked.

Nick squeezed my hand. 'I'm sure.'

Daniel's frown deepened. 'Just so we're clear. She sleeps in Matt's room and there's no more of this.' He leaned over the centre console and tapped on our joined hands.

I pulled my hand free. 'For God's sake, Daniel. He was just being nice.'

'Yeah, well, from now on he can be nice without the touching.' He lightly punched Nick on the arm. 'Got it?'

'Got it.'

I shook my head, trying not to think about how good it had felt to have Nick holding my hand. He was just trying to be nice, make me feel better. With everything I had just learned, I needed all the comfort I could get. It was an effort to drag my thoughts away from what might be happening to Angel back at the estate to focus on what I needed to do next.

'I'm going to need clothes,' I said, 'and my toothbrush and stuff.'

'Nick, can you drop me off at the mechanic's?' Daniel asked. 'I'll wait there until my car is ready and then go home and pack a bag for Andie. In fact, I think I'll pack one for me too, along with my swag. I can sleep on the floor in Matt's room, and keep Andie company.'

'Sure thing, Dan,' said Nick with a quick smile.

I rolled my eyes, convinced Daniel wouldn't be worried about keeping me company if I was going to be spending the night at a girl's house. Not that I was disappointed to have him staying with me at Nick's. I hardly knew Nick, and staying at his house, even if I was sleeping in another room, was bound to be awkward. No, it would be much better to have Daniel there as well. Besides, sticking together would give us more time to brainstorm how we were going to free Angel.

When we reached the mechanic's, Daniel's car was ready

to go. He headed home to pack our things, while Nick took me to his place, with a detour to get some takeout for a late lunch.

Balancing the drink tray in one hand, holding a bag of burgers and fries in the other, I waited for Nick to unlock the front door of his flat.

Nick gestured for me to walk in ahead of him. 'Welcome to my castle.'

I stepped inside, my left arm brushing against his chest as I walked into the lounge of the small flat, careful not to trip on any of the electrical cords snaking over the floor. Eyes wide, I surveyed the large television set up along one wall and the array of games consoles in front of it, with dozens of game cases scattered around the floor.

'Matt's a gamer.' Nick grimaced. 'Big on playing, not so much with the packing up.' He shot forward and used his feet to clear a path, so I could walk over to the small round dining table set in a nook off the kitchen and set our lunch down.

'You don't play?' I sat down and rested my arms on the table, aware of how little I knew about the guy who had been a constant source of support since my world fell apart.

'Not as much as Matt. It's all he does, apart from work, and I'm pretty sure the only reason he does work is to get money to buy even more games. He's got just about every one there is, and all the different consoles to play them on.'

'Sounds like a lonely life.'

'Yeah, I guess. Definitely not the kind of life I'm interested in.' He sat opposite me, intent gaze fixed on my face.

Warmth flooded my cheeks and I busied myself taking the food out of the paper bag. 'Daniel should be here soon. Shouldn't take him long to pack us an overnight bag each and grab his swag.'

'I'm starving,' said Nick as he picked up one of the

burgers. He took it out of the box. 'He'd better hurry up, or his food is going to be stone cold by the time he gets here.'

I took the top off my burger and added a layer of fries to it. Then I replaced the top and bit into it. I looked up to find Nick watching me. I swallowed my mouthful and wiped my lips.

'What's wrong?'

'Nothing, I've just never seen anyone put fries in their burger before.'

'You should try it.'

Nick did as I suggested, giving me the thumbs up after his first bite. 'Not bad. Not bad at all.'

We ate in silence, washing our burger and fries down with soft drink, and there was still no sign of Daniel by the time we finished. Then my mobile rang.

'It's Daniel,' I said after checking the caller ID. I accepted the call. 'What's taking you so long? Your lunch is getting cold.'

'They're watching the house. That orderly who tried to grab you back at the estate is sitting in a white van across the road. If I leave, he might follow me.'

The food I had just eaten threatened to reappear and I swallowed several times to keep it down. 'You're sure it's him?'

My voice was little more than a whisper, but it was enough to make Nick shoot out of his seat and come around the table to kneel at my side. I hit the speaker button on my phone, so he could hear Daniel's response.

'I'm sure, and he's brought a friend who's just as big and mean-looking along for the ride.'

I took a deep breath. 'They can't watch you forever. Sit tight for now and come over when they leave.'

'I don't like it, leaving you there all alone.'

'She's not alone. She has me,' said Nick.

'That's what worries me. Remember what I said. Keep your hands off my sister.'

Nick looked down at his hands, which currently rested on my leg. 'Sure, mate, whatever you say.'

I said goodbye to Daniel and placed my phone on the table. My hands were shaking. 'They're not going to stop looking for me, are they? Sooner or later they'll find me.'

Nick stood up, tugging me to my feet with him. He wrapped his arms around me and pulled me against his body, his chin resting on the top of my head. 'I won't let them take you. I won't.'

I closed my eyes, listening to the steady beat of his heart beneath my cheek. 'Maybe I should let them take me. At least that way I'd be with Angel.'

'No, don't think like that.' Nick shifted position and I tilted my head back, so I could meet his eyes.

'She's been locked up in that place for fifteen years, all alone, while I got to live my life out here. It's not fair. I should be with her.'

'You will be, when we get her out.'

'What if we don't? What if her doctor is right and we can't get her released?'

'We will find a way. I promise.'

I gazed up at Nick, the warmth of his body seeping into mine, chasing away the chill that had set in during Daniel's call. He smiled, dimples appearing on either side of his mouth. Cradled in his arms, conscious of his hands on the small of my back, I gave a sigh. I licked my lips, and then froze when Nick's gaze zeroed in on my mouth. His dimples vanished as he dipped his head, bringing it down until his lips brushed lightly against mine.

His mouth hovered over mine, barely touching. I held my breath, and then I moved, parting my lips and pressing them firmly against his. Nick took full advantage, drawing me in even closer as he deepened the kiss.

I moved my hands to his shoulders, clutching them as Nick's mouth coursed over mine, tasting, teasing. Heat blossomed low in my belly and I moaned, head spinning as I pressed my body against his, wanting to connect with every inch of him, not sure what it was I was asking for, only knowing I needed it.

Nick grasped my hips and pulled my lower body against his. He moved his right hand down to cup my left thigh, He lifted my leg and then thrust his hips forward, pelvis rocking against mine. I gasped and pulled my mouth from his, breathing heavily.

'Nick … I can't,' I said, hardly able to hear my voice over the thundering beat of my heart.

Nick let go so suddenly I almost fell. He stepped backwards, hands pulling at his thick hair. 'Oh my God, Andie, I am so sorry. Please don't hate me.' His chest heaved, breathing evidently as out of control as mine.

I shook my head. 'Why would I hate you?'

'I was practically mauling you.'

'What? No. I may not be experienced when it comes to kissing, but I'm pretty sure it takes two.'

'What do you mean, you're not experienced?'

I shrugged, not meeting his eyes. 'Well, it's not like I've had a lot of time for boyfriends, what with being sedated for most of my life. Since I left home I've been focused on weaning myself off the tablets and getting good marks at university.'

'That was your first kiss?' He groaned. 'Daniel is going to kill me.'

'This has got nothing to do with Daniel. This is between you and me. And yes, technically, that was my first kiss. But it's no big deal, right? It was just a kiss.' A mind-blowing kiss, for me at least, but I was sure it wouldn't have meant anything to Nick. With his looks and easy charm, he would have had plenty of kissing experience to compare with my first attempt.

Nick narrowed his eyes. 'On a scale of one to ten, that was a twelve. It most definitely was not just a kiss.'

'Oh,' I said, dropping my eyes, pleasantly surprised. I took a deep breath, working up the nerve to close the gap between us and see if a second kiss was just as mind blowing.

'But it should never have happened. I promised Daniel I wouldn't touch you. He'll never forgive me if he finds out I kissed you.'

I swallowed heavily, forcing myself to meet his eyes, ignoring the sinking feeling in the pit of my stomach. 'He doesn't need to find out, and it won't happen again. It can't. You're Daniel's best friend. I'm his sister. It would never work. Besides, I need to focus on getting Angel back. I don't have time to think about boys or kissing.'

'If that's what you want, we can forget it ever happened.'

'It is,' I said, the sinking feeling reaching out and leaching all emotion out of my voice. I turned away from Nick and gathered up the debris from our lunch, back stiff as I fought not to cry. I focused on the last image I'd had of Angel, terrified, strapped to a bed.

I had to free her.

Nothing else mattered.

12

Nick and I spent the rest of the day in relative silence, watching movies with lots of explosions and not a hint of romance, sitting as far apart as the couch allowed. Daniel rang twice, checking in and to let me know our flat was still being watched.

After the third movie, unable to stop yawning, I stood. 'I'm going to call it a night.'

'Sure,' said Nick as he also stood. 'Matt's room is this way.' He led me down the hall and stopped at the first door on the left. He opened it and poked his head inside, making me jump back when he recoiled and slammed the door shut a second later.

'Change of plan. You can sleep in my room. I'll take the couch,' he said with a sheepish grin. 'Matt's room is not fit for human habitation. I'm pretty sure something died in there.'

'Oh, okay, but you don't have to give up your bed. I can sleep on the couch.'

'No way. You look beat. You need a good night's sleep. I'm taking the couch, and that's final.'

Too tired to argue, I nodded and followed as he moved on to the next door. I stepped inside Nick's room and smiled when I spotted all the books crammed into a bookcase resting against the wall opposite the bed. More books were piled on top of it and I picked up one of them to inspect the cover. It depicted a helicopter with what looked like an enormous dragon chasing it, flame shooting out of its mouth.

'It's a good book. You should read it,' said Nick as he

rummaged in a tall chest of drawers next to the bookcase. 'Here, you can wear these tonight.' He held out a T-shirt and a pair of satin boxers. 'Don't worry, they're clean.'

'It's fine. I can sleep in my clothes.' While I appreciated his offer, to wear his clothes would imply a level of intimacy I wanted to avoid after the scene earlier.

'Jeans are never comfortable to sleep in. Believe me, I've done it.' He thrust the clothes at me. 'Please, I'd hate to think you were tossing and turning all night because you weren't comfortable.'

His expression was so earnest, I found myself taking the clothes despite my misgivings. I dropped my eyes, slipping past him to go to the bathroom to change. Once I was dressed, I folded my jeans and T-shirt and hung them over my arm as I stared at my reflection in the mirror. My long hair had slipped free of the knot at the back of my neck and now spilled halfway down my back in a messy tangle. I smoothed it as best I could, twisting it into a plait, but it wasn't the state of my hair that drew my gaze.

Nick's shirt skimmed my thighs while the boxers rode low on my hips, the material of both soft against my skin. Even though they were clean, a faint trace of his scent lingered in the air, making me feel like I was enveloped in his arms and not his clothes. My cheeks flushed as I remembered his kiss and my body's reaction to it. Before I left the bathroom, I splashed water on my face, hoping no trace of the turbulent emotions swirling through my body would be evident when I faced him again.

He stood just inside his bedroom, waiting for me. My stomach dipped, a tingle sweeping over me at the sight of him. He'd also changed into T-shirt and boxers, leaving his tanned arms and legs bare. His long, muscular legs were covered with dark hairs and the well-worn shirt clearly showed the definition of his torso.

His dimples appeared as he took in the view of me in my borrowed clothes, his clothes, and his eyes filled with an appreciation that had me flushing all over again. I tore my gaze away from his as I placed my dirty clothes on the end of the bed.

I straightened, clearing my throat as I shot a quick glance his way. 'I should probably get to bed. It's been a big day and tomorrow could be even bigger.' Not that I felt all that tired now, every inch of me thrumming at his nearness.

'Of course,' said Nick. 'Goodnight. Sleep well.'

'Goodnight,' I said, managing a small smile as he left the room and closed the door behind him.

Relieved to be finally alone, I switched off the bedroom light and slipped between the sheets, determined not to think about Nick. I lay on my back, eyes closed, waiting until my heart rate had eased before reaching out for Angel. But as earlier in the car, the impenetrable wall blocked my way. After several attempts I gave up and rolled onto my side, wiggling until I was comfortable. Nick's scent wrapped around me, rising from the pillow and bedding. I breathed deeply and let myself drift off to sleep.

An unfamiliar nightmare gripped me. Even as I thrashed on the bed, desperate to avoid the clutches of the brutish orderly as I fought to get to Angel, part of me noted this was indeed a nightmare, not a memory or a vision. But it still terrified me to see Angel strapped to a bed while a middle-aged woman in a lab coat stabbed her repeatedly with a syringe. Electrodes clung to every inch of flesh exposed by Angel's white nightgown and dozens of machines whirred as needles scratched out the data they extracted.

I whimpered, feeling Angel's pain each time the syringe pierced her flesh, fear choking my throat as the machines increased their tempo.

Then a warm hand stroked my face and Nick's soothing voice dragged me free from the nightmare. He slipped into bed behind me, one arm going under my body to pull me against his chest. He slung his other arm over my waist, tucking me even more firmly against him. My shudders eased, and I relaxed in his embrace as he continued to murmur in my ear that everything was going to be okay.

Eyes closed, safe in Nick's arms, I let sleep take me once more.

Hours later, sunlight streamed through a gap in the curtains and teased me awake. I didn't want to move, my body so relaxed, all I wanted to do was burrow even more deeply into the warmth surrounding me and go back to sleep. Then the warmth moved, and my eyes shot open.

Breath held, I looked at the tanned arm that held me so tenderly, suddenly conscious of the heavy leg draped over mine. Nick was spooned around me, each breath he took pressing his chest against my back, his right arm slung over my waist. Carefully, slowly, I eased myself forward to create a gap between our bodies. Nick sighed in his sleep and rolled forward, closing the gap.

I froze when his right hand slid under my shirt to cup my left breast. Long fingers kneaded the tender flesh. One of his fingers brushed against my nipple and I gasped at the heady sensation that shot through my body. I pushed his arm away and clambered out of bed and crossed my arms over my chest, shaking as I looked at Nick.

He rolled onto his back, blinking sleepily up at me, hair all mussed. He gave me a sweet smile. 'Hey.'

I didn't respond, couldn't say a word, the memory of his intimate touch stilling my tongue.

Nick frowned and sat up, scratching at his head. 'I realise how this looks but it was perfectly innocent, I swear. You had a nightmare and I was comforting you. I was going to head back to the couch, but I guess I fell asleep. But nothing happened. I promise.'

My eyes widened. He didn't realise he'd had his hand on my breast. I exhaled, closed my eyes and took one long breath after another. Okay, I could handle this. I was an adult.

I opened my eyes and attempted a smile. 'I was just surprised. I'm not used to waking up with someone else in my bed.'

'Me either,' said Nick, both dimples on display.

I didn't believe him for a second, not with how good he looked with the sheets tangled around his body, eyes heavy-lidded from sleep. But I didn't say anything as I scooted around the bed to grab my clothes.

'I'm going to get dressed,' I said as I bolted from the room.

I'd barely taken two steps when someone banged on the front door.

'Open up, Nick.'

I walked to the front door and unlocked it to let Daniel in. A backpack on each shoulder, he brushed past me and entered the lounge.

'Where's Nick?' Daniel frowned at me as he dumped the backpacks on the floor. 'What are you wearing?'

'I didn't have pyjamas, so Nick gave me these to wear,' I said as I knelt and unzipped one of the backpacks, smiling when I recognised the contents.

'Morning,' said Nick as he walked down the hall. He was dressed in jeans and a clean shirt. 'I guess this means your shadows gave up.'

'The van was gone when I woke up this morning. Thought I'd better get over here, and give Andie her stuff.' Daniel's eyes narrowed as he looked from Nick to me, and then to the couch covered with blankets and a pillow. 'Make sure she was okay.'

Nick frowned. 'You're sure you weren't followed?'

Daniel gave a nod. 'I was careful. There was no sign of the white van, and I took evasive action just in case they were following me, to make sure.'

'Evasive action? You watch too many movies,' I said as I stood with a bundle of clean clothes and toiletries in my arms. 'Do you mind if I have a shower?' I asked Nick, pleased my voice was steady, although I avoided making eye contact.

'Go right ahead. I put a towel out for you last night.'

'Thanks.' I scooted past him, and headed to the bathroom, refusing to think about anything other than how we were going to free Angel. She was my priority, not Daniel's too-handsome-for-his-own-good best friend, no matter how appealing he might be or how his kiss had blown my mind. Besides, he wasn't interested in me, at least not enough to want to jeopardise his friendship with my brother.

Ten minutes later, showered and refreshed, I returned to the lounge to find Nick on his own, the door to the flat wide open. I willed my breathing to settle down as I approached him.

'Where's Daniel?'

'He's getting his swag,' Nick said as he stepped closer to me, chocolate brown eyes intent on mine. 'Listen, about yesterday, and last night. I don't want you to get the wrong idea.'

'No, it's fine. I understand. It didn't mean anything. You're the first aid guy, you fix things. I get it.' I bit my bottom lip, willing him to believe me, willing myself not to wish for anything more.

'No, you don't get it.' Nick reached out and caressed my cheek. 'What I'm trying to say is that it does mean something. It means everything, at least it does to me, and I'm hoping you feel the same.'

I sucked in a breath, all rational thought blown away by

the realisation he was interested in me, and I could no longer pretend I wasn't feeling the same. All the lectures to myself about Angel being my priority had been a cover, a shield to protect me from being hurt by possible rejection. Freeing my sister was the most important thing in the world to me, but the feelings I was developing for Nick were not going to go away just because the timing wasn't ideal.

Before I could tell him how I felt, that this was the start of something amazing, I heard a noise and turned to see Daniel standing in the doorway. His eyes were wide, nostrils flaring, and my stomach fell.

He must have heard Nick's words. He was going to be furious with me, with Nick.

Daniel stumbled forward, shoved by someone behind him. He fell to his knees just inside the doorway. Mouth open, I stared in horror at the huge orderly as he stepped inside, three men at his back. Two of them were dressed in black uniforms, with a security badge on the shirt pockets. The other was dressed like an orderly and had a syringe in one hand.

'That's her. She's the one we want,' said the huge orderly.

'You're not taking her.' Nick pushed me behind him. 'I won't let you.'

'Son,' said one of the security guards. 'You don't have a choice.' He moved forward and grabbed hold of Nick, wrenching him away from me.

The other security guard hauled Daniel to his feet, twisting his arm behind his back to subdue him.

Nick struggled to break the security guard's grip on his arm, swinging a punch that landed on his jaw.

'Son of a bitch.' The security guard lashed out, hitting Nick so hard he was knocked backward and landed on the couch. The guard was on him in a second, pinning him down.

'Andie, run.'

Freed from my paralysis by Nick's shout, I dashed through the lounge, making for the front door. But the huge orderly blocked my path, arms spread wide. I pivoted, and raced down the hall, looking for the back door. But someone grabbed the back of my shirt and wrenched me backwards. Thick arms encircled me, pinning my arms at my sides, trapping me.

'Hurry up and jab her.' The orderly spun me around, lifting my feet off the ground as he called out to his accomplice. The second orderly, after a panicked look at where Nick and Daniel were fighting to get free of the security guards, scooted forward with the syringe raised.

I kicked back at the legs of the orderly holding me, but all that made him do was grunt. The other one reached my side, syringe aimed at my shoulder.

'Ouch.' A sharp sting was immediately followed by a cold sensation when the drug flowed into me.

The first orderly tossed me toward the second one. 'Quick, get her in the van. I'll help sort out these guys.'

I tried to protest, to fight, but a strange lethargy swept over me. When the orderly tugged my arm, I flowed along behind him. I lifted my feet high with each step, sure the ground was rising. I blinked at the brightness as we emerged from the house and tried to focus on the white van the orderly was leading me to, a security car parked behind it.

I frowned, shaking my head as I fought to remember something, something bad about the white van. I didn't want to get inside it, but couldn't remember why.

'Climb in the back and lie on the stretcher,' said the orderly, his voice ringing in my head.

I clambered through the open side door and looked at the stretcher clamped in place by brackets in the floor. I lay down on it, finding it harder and harder to keep my eyes open as I felt my arms and legs being moved. Tight bands wrapped around me, securing me in place as I gave up on staying awake, letting the encroaching darkness swallow me whole.

13

The smell hit me first, strong, antiseptic, like an industrial strength version of the hand sanitiser Joyce made everyone use any time they entered her house. I forced my eyes open only to slam them immediately shut to block out the bright light streaming down on me. A pounding in my head made it hard to think, to remember what had happened. I swallowed and winced when the movement hurt my throat. I was so thirsty. I needed water and painkillers for my raging headache.

Where was I? What had happened to me?

I opened my eyes the tiniest bit, allowing them to gradually become accustomed to the light. Tears streamed from them as they slowly and painfully adjusted. When my vision cleared I gazed around me.

I was in a large room with white walls, strapped to a bed, just like the one I had seen in my vision of Angel. There was an empty bed on my right, and a thick black curtain ran across the width of the room on the other side of it.

I was in the Wood Estate.

'Good, you're awake. Now we can begin testing you.' An older woman with hazel eyes and dark-brown hair tied up in a ponytail leaned over me. The badge on her lab coat read 'Dr Joanna Wood'. She had two electrodes with wires coming out of them in her hands and she placed them on my temples. Then she turned to the machine the wires were attached to and flicked switches.

I tried to talk, to ask her what she was doing, but my mouth was so dry all that came out was a croak.

Dr Wood picked up a white cup with a straw sitting in it. 'Here, this will help soothe your throat.' She brought it closer and placed the tip of the straw against my lips.

I slurped up the water, closing my eyes as the liquid filled my mouth. It hurt to swallow at first and then it got better, but Dr Wood took the cup away long before my thirst was satisfied.

'That's enough for now,' she said. 'We don't want you getting sick. You can have more after your tests are completed.'

'What tests?' My voice still didn't sound like my own, but at least I could now talk, even if I could only manage a few words at a time.

'The tests are to see if you have the same abilities as your remarkable sister.'

'Abilities?'

The creases around Dr Wood's eyes deepened when she smiled. 'Angel is psychic. She can see certain events before they occur, as well as being able to move objects with the power of her mind.'

My eyes went wide. 'That's not possible. Stuff like that only happens in movies.'

'I have spent the last fifteen years studying your sister, testing her and collecting data. I can assure you, her abilities are very real. She is not as powerful as I would like, but still a perfect case study. I'm hoping you will prove to be just as useful. When I am ready to release my findings, having two of you as evidence will create more interest in my work.'

'I'm not psychic. I can't do any of that stuff.' I struggled to sit up, to tear the electrodes from my temples, but couldn't move. I was strapped down, just as Angel had been in my last vision of her.

Dr Wood leaned over me, a cold smile on her thin lips. 'I sincerely hope that is not the case. After all the effort I have gone to, cultivating a friendship with your guardians, working on your aunt's insecurities, to get you here, I'm going to be very disappointed if I find out you're worthless to me.' Her smile disappeared. 'Don't disappoint me.'

I shuddered under her glacial glare, latching on to her words as a way to distract her. 'What do you mean, about my aunt?'

'Unable to have children of her own, Joyce saw you and your brother as the means to create the perfect family. While she was easily convinced to sign your sister over to me, she refused to part with you.' She gave me a sly look. 'Your recurring nightmares certainly made her regret that decision. But by then it was too late to ship you off to me without anyone noticing.'

She shrugged. 'She did allow me to assess you, but as you displayed no psychic abilities at the time I did not push it. Still, I did get her to sign the paperwork before you came of age, just in case. And it seems I was right to do so. Joyce tells me you have been having visions of your sister, visions that led you here.'

'None of this makes sense. You couldn't have known Angel was psychic when she was three. Why did you want us?'

'I knew exactly what your sister was. Your parents brought her to me when she was two, after she began exhibiting unusual behaviours. On our first session, when I was alone with her, she made a toy she wanted fall from the shelf. I spent the rest of the session confirming what I suspected and then advised your parents to sign her over to me.'

She grimaced. 'They refused to even consider the idea. I did everything I could, warned them she would become increasingly unstable without twenty-four-hour care, but they were adamant. Then they died, and your aunt signed the papers at once. A mute child did not fit her image of the perfect family.'

I shook my head, unable to comprehend how this woman could lock a child away for fifteen years, even if she was psychic. 'Why do you care? What difference does it make if Angel can move things with her mind? It doesn't mean anything.'

Fire flared in her eyes. 'It means everything. Everything.'

Her mouth screwed up in a snarl. 'I was set to revolutionise the way we understand the human brain and what it is capable of. Then a little cheat took it all away from me, tricked me into believing he had genuine psychic abilities. After my announcement, when he was exposed as a fake, my reputation was ruined. I had to flee Sydney, start over with a new name, in a different career, but I am not going to spend the rest of my life wiping the noses of snotty little brats who can't handle the pressures of the real world.'

She took several deep breaths, fists clenched at her sides as she glared at me. 'I will prove to those people who ridiculed my research that I was right all along. And you and your sister are going to help me do it.'

She turned away to pick up some cards twice the size of her hands, expression smooth when she faced me once more. 'I couldn't risk going public again with only one test subject, and unfortunately none of the other patients I have treated here at the estate have shown any evidence of psychic abilities. But once I have confirmed which abilities you possess I will finally be able to complete my research. To that end, I'm going to hold up a card and you will tell me what is on the other side. Let's begin.'

She held up the first card and looked at me expectantly. I stared blankly at it, with no idea what image was on the other side.

Dr Wood frowned. 'I need you to take this seriously.

Concentrate. What do you see?'

'Where is my sister? I want to see Angel.'

'The card, Andrea.'

'I have no idea. I told you, I'm not psychic.'

'Impossible. You have been having visions of your sister. You must have a psychic ability. You're just not trying hard enough. Perhaps this will persuade you.' She reached into a pocket and pulled out a slim black device with two stubby prongs sticking out of one end.

She placed the prongs against my leg, never taking her eyes off me. I heard a low whirring noise coming from the device a split second before pain zapped into my leg.

I screamed, body jolting as the current ripped through me, barely registering when she lifted the device. Muscle spasms kept me twitching long after the pain subsided. It took a few minutes before I was able to focus my eyes on Dr Wood.

I glared at her. 'Is this what you do to Angel? Torture her? Make her read cards for you?'

'If I were you, I would be more concerned with my own situation. Unless you want a repeat,' she waved the device in my face before putting it back in her pocket, 'I suggest you start cooperating. What do you see?' She held up a card.

I met her eyes, not even looking at the card. 'Angel.'

'Do not test me, Andrea. You will not like the result.' She thrust the card forward.

'Angel. Angel. Angel.' I kept going, getting louder and louder.

Dr Wood pulled the device out of her pocket and zapped me again, but this time I was prepared. I clenched my jaw and tensed my body, riding out the pain. As soon as I could speak I started again. 'Angel. Angel.'

After she zapped me for the third time I was only able to whisper Angel's name. Eyes closed, I waited for her to punish me, sure I would black out this time.

'Andie.' Angel's voice, even fainter than mine, sounded in my head. 'Can you hear me?'

I struggled to open my eyes. 'Angel,' I sighed as I focused on the room, looking for her. But I was still alone with Dr Wood, who stood with her back to me.

She was leaning over the machine I was hooked up to, peering at the readout as the needle whirred across the paper.

'Angel,' I said again, a little louder.

'I need you, Andie. Find me.'

'I'm trying,' I said.

Angel's presence faded, and I closed my eyes, worn out by the effort to communicate with her.

'What did you just do?'

I forced my eyes open and peered up at Dr Wood. She held a sheet of paper in her hands and shoved it in front of my face. 'These spikes, here, indicate considerable brain activity.' She pointed at the printout. 'What did you do?'

I smiled and closed my eyes as I said, 'Angel.'

'Damn it, Andrea. I need you to work with me. I don't like hurting you, but I will if that's what it takes.'

I lay silent, holding myself still when I felt her press the black device against my leg. It took every ounce of courage I had not to flinch, to stifle the cry threatening to burst out of me in anticipation of being zapped again.

14

'If I take you to see your sister, will you tell me what you did to make the readout spike?' Dr Wood stared at me, a deep frown creasing her brow.

I expelled the air from my lungs in a rush. 'Yes.'

The pressure on my leg eased and I felt her undoing the straps that held me down.

'Get up,' she said.

I opened my eyes and tried to sit up. Impossible. My limbs wouldn't obey me, the muscles twitching uselessly as I willed them to work.

'If you want to see her, get up now or our deal is off.' She stood at the end of the bed, the device she'd zapped me with in one hand.

I glared at her, using my hatred as fuel. I lurched into a sitting position and swung my legs off the bed. I stood, gripping the rail to keep myself upright when my legs threatened to collapse under me. I locked my knees and focused on the pain, on overcoming it, and took a step, followed by another.

I reached the end of the bed as Dr Wood moved to the door and held it open for me. 'Hurry up, before I change my mind.'

With a deep breath, I let go of the bed and shuffled over to the door, my footing surer the farther I went. I passed the doctor and then stood in the hallway, looking to the right. Angel was that way, somewhere below me, but I waited for Dr Wood to take the lead, not wanting her to know I could sense my sister's presence now I was no longer distracted by fear and pain.

I hobbled along behind the doctor, careful not to show I was finding it easier to walk, movement working out the kinks in my muscles. She slowed her pace to match mine and led me to an elevator. Inside, she tugged on a chain around her neck and pulled it out from beneath her shirt. A key dangled on the end.

The keypad showed six floors, three aboveground and three below. The display panel said we were on L2, the second underground level. Dr Wood placed the key in a slot beside the keypad and turned it before pressing L3.

The elevator descended slowly. When we reached L3 the doors slid open and Dr Wood indicated for me to step out ahead of her.

I entered a short corridor with two doors on either side. Dr Wood prodded me in the back and I moved forward, bare feet making no noise on the concrete floor. The first two doors were open, allowing me a glimpse of white walls and empty beds. Then I reached the last two. The door on my right was open, also showing an empty room. The door on my left was closed, and I stepped up to the glass window set in the top half and peered inside, my breath catching.

Angel was curled on her side, back to the door, a manacle around one ankle with a length of chain attached that was anchored to the wall at the end of her bed. She rolled over and stared at me, a smile on her face. She got off the bed and walked toward the door, coming as close as the chain would allow her. She stretched out her hand, trying to bridge the gap between us.

'You've seen her. Now tell me how you made the machine spike.'

'Please, let me in, let me go to her.' I faced Dr Wood, tears in my eyes.

'After you tell me what I want to know.'

'We haven't seen each other for fifteen years. Just give me five minutes with her and I promise I will tell you everything.' I wrung my hands, desperate for her to agree.

'Tell me now, or I will make sure this is the last time you and Angel ever see each other. I'll lock you in the room next door, so close but forever apart. The rooms are soundproof. You won't even be able to talk to her.'

'Please. I'm begging you. All I'm asking for is five minutes. That's all.'

I could tell my pleas were having no effect. If I had anything interesting to tell her about the spike on the readout, I would do it in a heartbeat. But I knew it hadn't been from me. It had been from Angel reaching out to me. I was not psychic and once Dr Wood realised that I knew her interest in me would vanish, along with any chance I had to see Angel.

A low buzz sounded close by and Dr Wood reached into her pocket to pull out a mobile phone. 'Yes, what is it?'

She listened a moment, and then stiffened. 'All right. I'll be there in a minute.'

She put the phone away and glared at me. 'You had better be worth this.' She punched a code into the keypad on Angel's door and it beeped as the light switched from red to green. She pushed it open.

'Get in.'

I walked inside and stood in front of Angel, resisting the urge to hug her until I knew we were alone. The door clanged shut behind me and I peeked over my shoulder to make sure Dr Wood wasn't watching.

'She's gone,' Angel's voice said in my head.

I turned around and stepped closer to Angel, and for the first time in fifteen years we touched.

Our arms wrapped around each other and a brilliant light flared, bursting out of Angel's body and into mine, I gasped, body shaking as wave after wave of energy swept through me.

Tears streamed down my face in its wake and when the light faded, I looked into Angel's eyes.

'I remember,' I said. 'I remember everything.'

Images filled my head; playing with Angel in our room, laughing as Dad chased Daniel, Angel and me around the backyard with Mum watching on, Daniel pushing Angel on the swing while I waited for my turn, the fire that ripped our world apart and separated me from my twin sister.

My heart ached, even as it rejoiced that we were finally together again.

'You found me,' said Angel, her voice in my head stronger and clearer than it had ever been.

'I'm so sorry I forgot you,' I sobbed into her hair, clutching her tight.

'It's okay. It wasn't your fault.' She drew back and gazed into my eyes, cheeks wet with tears. 'You're here now, that's all that matters.'

Her laughter was light and carefree in my head. 'I can't believe it worked. I've been trying to contact you for years. But I couldn't get through. It was as though you were surrounded by a thick fog that muffled my voice, until yesterday.'

'The sedatives,' I said. 'I've been weaning myself off them.' I shuddered, horrified to think, if I had given in to temptation the night before last, Angel would never have been able to contact me. I'd come so close to giving in. I hugged her even tighter, relishing the bond linking us.

'Dr Wood uses sedatives on me too, to make sure I can't run away. It dulls my abilities though, so she can't use them when she wants to run tests on me. She used to let me stay upstairs, with the other patients. But after my last escape attempt, she moved me down here permanently, to make it even harder.'

I frowned. 'She told me she wants to use us to get back at

the people who ruined her career, years ago, in Sydney.'

'I know. She talks about it all the time, standing up to them, showing them she was right and they were wrong. She hates them, and the boy who tricked her. She tests all the new patients, uses shock therapy on them if she can get away with it, all to see if they have psychic abilities like me. She's obsessed with finding more evidence to support her research and doesn't care who she has to hurt to get it.'

'She thinks I could be psychic too, but I'm not. I can't do the things you can.'

Angel tilted her head on the side, eyes closed. 'I can sense power in you but you're right, it's different to mine.' She opened her eyes, frowning. 'It's as though you're a reservoir, filled with energy but with no way of accessing it. But when I'm touching you I can access it, make myself stronger.'

'If she discovers that, she'll never let us go. We have to get out of here.' I released Angel and moved over to the bed, grabbing hold of the chain and tugging on it, panic lending me strength. The screw bolting the chain to the wall didn't budge. I tugged even harder, the chain digging into my fingers, cutting off my circulation. But I wouldn't, couldn't give up. Dr Wood could return at any minute. We had to get away.

'It's okay.' Angel put her hands over mine. 'Now that you're here, I can break the lock. Sit.'

I dropped the chain and sat on the bed, fighting to steady my breathing as she took a seat beside me. Then she pulled up her leg and rested her foot between us. She took my free hand and placed it on the manacle before putting her hand on top.

'Concentrate on the lock. Block out everything else, and I'll do the rest.'

My breathing settled as I stared at the lock, willing it to open.

Energy sizzled in the air around me, emanating from Angel. The hair on my arms rose and I felt a pull inside my head, behind my eyes, as she drew on … something. I couldn't see what she was doing with all the energy she harnessed but I could sense its presence when she focused it on the lock.

With a sharp click, the lock fell open. When the connection Angel had forged in my head dissipated I sagged onto the bed, sweat beading on my forehead.

I leaned back against the wall as Angel slipped the manacle off her ankle and rubbed the red, raised marks it had left on the skin. She stood and held out her hand to me. 'We need to go now. Dr Wood has sent one of the orderlies to take you back to the testing room.'

I took her hand and pushed myself off the bed. My legs were shaky, but they quickly stabilised. We stood, hand in hand, in front of the door and focused on the lock.

I sagged in Angel's arms once she had channelled our combined energy to open the door. 'How come you're not exhausted, like me?'

'I've had more practice. Dr Wood makes me train every day, but I couldn't do this without you.'

I pushed myself upright. 'Let's do it.'

Angel kept an arm around my waist, supporting me as we walked toward the elevator.

The doors started to open when we were still three metres away and through the widening gap I could see the huge orderly with the greasy ponytail. His eyes widened when he realised we were loose. Angel waved her hand at the elevator doors and I felt a drain on my energy levels as they closed, trapping the orderly inside.

'I can't keep the doors closed for long. We'll have to take the stairs.'

She led me over to a fire exit beside the elevator. It was locked with a keypad and I braced myself for the drain as Angel worked to open it. But she didn't take anything from me. The door clicked open and she stumbled. It was my turn to support her as we moved into the stairwell, waiting for the click to signal the door had locked behind us before we started to climb.

Loud banging on the exit door on L3 came as we passed the door to L2. We pushed on, breathing heavily. My thigh and calf muscles burned, and I contemplated leaving the stairwell and taking the elevator when we reached L1.

'No,' Angel said before I could even suggest it. 'He is back in the elevator, on his way up. We need to go faster to beat him to the ground floor.'

With a groan, I pumped my legs harder, gritting my teeth as we tackled the last set of stairs. I sucked air in through my mouth when we reached the next landing and stumbled to the exit. There was no keypad on this side, luckily for us, as I didn't think either of us had enough energy left to open it. From here on we would have to rely on willpower alone.

I pushed the door open and Angel and I stepped into a small alcove. The elevator was to our right and the display read L1 and climbing.

Arms around one another's waists, we stumbled around the corner and into a large room filled with adolescents dressed in white nightgowns or pyjamas, some with robes over the top. They were scattered around the room, some of them reading as they reclined on comfortable couches, others playing computer games or watching television. It would have looked like a pyjama party in a dormitory, if not for the bars I could see on the windows.

Many of the patients stopped what they were doing and looked at us, some registering shock at seeing us.

'Angel.' Several of the older ones came over, worried frowns on their faces, just as the elevator in the alcove behind us gave a ding to signal it had reached the ground floor.

'Please,' I said. 'We need your help. Don't let him catch

us.' They nodded and brushed past us, moving to block the corridor. Angel and I continued through the room as more and more kids got up and joined the ones behind us.

I heard an angry bellow and peered over my shoulder. I could just make out the orderly's head as a sea of white-clad patients swarmed around him. He tried to shove his way through and I could hear cries of pain from those attempting to stop him.

I increased my speed, dragging Angel with me. On the other side of the large room was another corridor and we hurried into it. I could hear shouting up ahead and my heart leapt when I recognised Nick's and Daniel's voices. I couldn't hear what they were saying but just knowing they were close sent an adrenalin boost into my system.

The corridor ended in a right turn and as we took the corner I was sure we were only inches away from freedom. Then I saw the keypad-operated door that blocked our path, and my heart plummeted.

Angel and I halted in front of the door and she put her hand on the keypad. I could feel her drawing up energy and placed my hand over hers, desperate to give her everything I had. But it wasn't enough. We sagged to our knees, side by side, the door still locked.

I could hear Nick and Daniel, so close, only one stupid door between us. Tears pricked my eyes and I let them fall.

The door opened outwards and I fell to all fours, looking up into the startled eyes of a young woman in a nurse's uniform. She hastily backed up as Angel and I got to our feet, looking nervously behind her.

'Dr Wood,' she called out, voice trembling.

'Cynthia, can't you see I'm busy,' said the doctor from where she stood behind a large front counter.

'Andie!'

At Nick's shout the doctor's head swung around and her

eyes narrowed when they locked on mine. 'Who let you out?'

'We let ourselves out,' I said as Angel and I stumbled into the reception area. Nick was at my side within seconds, his arm snaking around my waist. I leaned into him as I watched Daniel grab some papers off the counter and stuff them down the front of his shirt before he ran over to us and put his arm around Angel.

'Where do you think you're going? These girls belong here. You have no right to take them.' Dr Wood glanced at the receptionist who sat open-mouthed behind the front counter. 'Call security. Now.'

With Nick supporting me, I ran to the front door and burst outside, with Angel and Daniel right behind. Nick's car was parked right in front of the entrance and I threw myself into the front passenger seat while Daniel and Angel dived into the back.

The two security guards who had helped kidnap me from Nick's flat raced from the building.

Nick bolted around the front of the car and then jumped into the driver's seat. He keyed the ignition as I used the button on the centre console to lock all the doors. Not a second too soon. The first security guard reached the car and smashed his baton against my window. The window cracked but didn't shatter. He pulled his arm back, ready to smash the window again. Nick floored the accelerator and the car sped off down the driveway.

Moments later we cleared the gates and the car skidded as Nick spun the wheel to takes us to the road that led back to town.

'We did it,' said Daniel, thumping the back of Nick's seat.

A flash of white caught my eye and I peered into the side mirror.

The white van, with the huge orderly at the wheel, was

only one hundred metres behind us, and steadily gaining.

'They're coming,' I said as I grabbed my seatbelt. 'Everybody buckle up.'

15

The van got closer, showing no signs of slowing down, and I could see Dr Wood in the passenger seat.

'Faster, Nick.'

'I'm going as fast as I can.' He didn't take his eyes off the road. 'Any faster and–'

The van slammed into the back of Nick's car with a bone-jarring thud. I was thrown forward, only the seatbelt stopping me from flying out of my seat. The car spun sideways and Nick fought to control it. The van rammed us again, side on, and the car careened off the road, sliding boot first into a ditch and coming to a shuddering halt.

I groaned, rubbing at my chest where the seat belt had dug in. My fingers fumbled to unbuckle it, to relieve the pressure on the bruising I could already feel forming.

'Are you okay?' Nick's hands brushed mine aside and he pushed the release.

I nodded and twisted to look in the back seat. 'Daniel? Angel? Are you guys okay?'

'Yes,' said Daniel, while Angel smiled at me. Then her eyes went wide.

The door on her side opened and the orderly reached in and grabbed hold of her arm. Daniel grabbed her other arm, but the orderly was too strong, relentless, as he dragged Angel out of the car. Daniel, still strapped in, frantically tugged at his seat belt.

I opened my door and got out of the car as the orderly pulled Angel toward the van. I launched myself at him, pummelling his back.

'Get away from her. Let her go.' I hit him again and again, to no avail. I jumped as high as I could and wrapped my arms around his thick neck, trying to choke him.

He let go of Angel and grabbed my arms, prying them away from his neck. He tossed me on the ground in front of him and reached down to take hold of my arm. He then moved to grab Angel again, but she scooted away from him on her hands and knees.

'Leave her alone.' Nick appeared beside me and threw a punch at the orderly's head.

When the orderly threw up his hand to block Nick's blow, I kicked him in the groin. He let out a strangled scream and let me go, crumpling to the ground. He curled up on his side, whimpering.

I hurried over to Angel as Daniel helped her to her feet. Nick joined us and together we stood and faced Dr Wood. She sneered at the fallen orderly as she stalked toward us. On the road behind the van, the security car came to a halt and the two guards jumped out.

Dr Wood gave us a cold smile. 'It's over. Andrea, Angel, get in the van before I call the police and have your brother and your friend arrested.'

'Like hell we're getting in the van. We are never going back to that place,' I said.

'Don't you understand? You don't have a choice. I have every legal right to keep you locked up forever. To do whatever I want to you.'

'We'll go to the media, get a lawyer.'

'If you go public the whole world will come after you and your sister, wanting to use your abilities. And lawyers cost money, which you four clearly do not have, and they wouldn't do you any good anyway. Your guardians signed your care over to me before you were of legal age, after I convinced them you were bound to have a psychotic episode if you stopped taking your medication. Not that they were hard to convince.'

'They are not my parents,' I said, clenching my jaw.

'Nonetheless, the paperwork is signed, and it is legally binding.'

'This paperwork?' Daniel reached under his shirt and pulled out the sheaf of papers I had seen him take from the front counter.

Dr Wood hissed. 'Give me those.'

'I don't think so.'

She spun around to the security guards. 'Get those papers. Now.'

Before the guards could move Angel snatched the papers out of Daniel's hand and moved closer to me, free hand reaching for mine.

'Now, Andie,' she said in my head.

I focused on the papers, striving to give Angel every ounce of energy I had. Pain flared in my head and I would have fallen if not for Nick's arm around my waist.

The papers burst into flames and Angel let them drop to the ground. Her hands were shaking, but she stood with her back straight as she faced Dr Wood. Angel's voice sounded in my head and I spoke the words she wanted all to hear.

'Go, leave us in peace, or you will also burn like the papers.'

A small flame appeared in Angel's palm and the security guards hastily backed away. She let the flame die down as the orderly pulled himself to his feet with a moan and hobbled over to his boss's side.

Dr Wood made to walk toward us, her mouth in a snarl, but stopped when Angel raised her hand again.

'You will torture us no more. Our lives are not yours to play with,' I said for her.

One of the security guards whispered in Dr Wood's ear,

all while keeping a wary eye on Angel. She glared at him, but whatever he said seemed to get through to her. With one final glare our way, she stalked back to the van and climbed into the passenger seat. The orderly hurried around to the driver's side and started the engine. In a spray of dust, the van shot back toward the Wood Estate.

The two security guards never took their eyes off Angel as they backed all the way to their car. Then they quickly followed the van.

The hand in mine went limp and Angel slumped forward, only Daniel's quick reflexes saving her from hitting the ground. Her eyes were closed; face deathly pale and respirations shallow.

'Angel.' I touched her face, willing her to open her eyes and look at me. She didn't respond. Fear flooded me, and I looked at Nick. 'We need to get her to a hospital.'

He gave a nod and helped Daniel carry her to the car. They laid her on the backseat and I climbed in with her, cradling her head on my lap.

The engine revved as Nick manoeuvred his car out of the ditch. We sped off and I stroked Angel's head all the way back to town, talking to her, telling her everything was going to be okay. She didn't move, just lay there barely breathing. I closed my eyes and tried to sense her presence, to find her in the darkness that had taken her from me. I found a faint glimmer, a tiny kernel of awareness getting smaller every second. I didn't see how it could survive for much longer.

My eyes shot open. 'Hurry, Nick. Please hurry.'

'Is she going to be okay?' Daniel asked, leaning over the back of the passenger seat.

'She expended so much energy to create the fire. There's nothing left to keep her going.' Tears streamed down my face. 'She's dying, Daniel. I can feel it.'

Tears formed in his eyes. 'But we just got her back. We

109

can't lose her again. There must be something we can do.'

'I don't know what to do. I don't know how to help her.'

'The hospital is four blocks away,' said Nick, his eyes meeting mine in the rear-view mirror. 'Just hold on for a few more minutes.'

I gazed at him, latching on to his words. Hold on. Could I do it?

I placed my hands on either side of Angel's head and closed my eyes, seeking that shrinking kernel of awareness floating alone in the dark. I thought back to the times Angel had drawn energy from me, where I had felt it in my head.

There. A light flared behind my eyes and I concentrated on sending it into Angel, wrapping it around the fading spark that contained her consciousness.

I slumped over her, faintly aware of Daniel calling my name. But I couldn't respond. Everything I had was focused on saving Angel, on sharing my light with her.

We were twins, we were part of each other, and together we were stronger.

With her awareness shielded by mine, I gave her time to heal, to come back to me. With each beat of our hearts her light grew stronger, her breathing deeper. In sync, we opened our eyes and gazed at each other, matching smiles of pure joy on our faces.

My tears fell on her forehead and I laughed as she crinkled her nose. I helped her to sit up. She closed her eyes again, still weak, and I let her rest.

'Take us home, Nick. We don't need to go to the hospital anymore,' I said, weary but content. 'Angel is going to be okay.'

Daniel gave me a watery smile and I reached forward to pat him on the shoulder as Nick did a U-turn.

We'd done it.

Angel was free.

I had my sister back, and no one was going to take her from me ever again.

16

I smoothed Angel's hair away from her face before backing out of my bedroom, quietly closing the door.

'She's asleep,' I said when I entered the lounge.

'I can't believe she's really here,' said Daniel, running his hands through his hair. 'All these years I thought she was dead, and instead that horrible woman was torturing her. I should have known something wasn't right. Your nightmares, pretending Angel never existed.' His voice cracked.

I moved over and gave him a hug. 'None of this was your fault. Joyce and Bill are the ones who stole Angel from us.'

'I still can't believe they would do something like that.'

'I can,' said Nick, sprawled on the couch. 'I already told Andie, your aunt is one scary lady. Between her and the crazy doctor, you didn't stand a chance.'

I let go of Daniel and sat beside Nick, reaching out to take his hand. 'Thank you, for everything you have done. If it wasn't for you, believing in me, I don't think we would have been able to save Angel.'

Nick tugged me closer and put his arm around me. 'I will always believe in you,' he said.

I looked into his eyes, caught by the intensity of his gaze. I sucked in a breath and leaned forward, anticipating the feel of his lips on mine.

'No way. You are not kissing my sister.' Daniel grabbed my arm and pulled me away from Nick.

I stumbled to my feet and faced Daniel, tugging my arm free. 'That is not your decision to make.'

'What? Are you saying you want him to kiss you?'

I didn't look at Nick. 'That is something I need to discuss with him, alone.' I pointed down the hall. 'Go check on Angel, please.'

'You just said she was asleep, and no way am I leaving the two of you alone.' He glared at Nick. 'You are not allowed to date my sister. Not happening.'

Nick stood and put his arm around my waist, drawing me to him. 'Sorry, Dan. You're my friend, and I'd hate for this to ruin our friendship, but I am going to date Andie. If she'll have me.'

He shifted me round so I stood facing him. 'Andrea Sherman, I'm crazy about you. You're remarkable, strong, fearless, amazing, and I want to give us a chance. What do you say?'

My smile was so big, he could have no doubt about my response, but I told him anyway. 'I'm crazy about you too, Nick Foster.'

I never got the chance to say anything more. His mouth covered mine and I lost myself in the taste of his lips. A long time later he lifted his head and we grinned at each other. I remembered Daniel and looked over to where he was pulling at his hair.

'Seriously guys, if this is going to work you can't do that in front of me ever again,' he said.

'So, you're okay with this, with us?' I waved a hand at Nick and me, still with our arms wrapped around each other.

'I guess I have to be. If I learned one thing from what we've gone through this weekend, it's not to mess with my little sister. Either of my little sisters. You made fire appear, out of nowhere. I can't even begin to imagine how you did that.'

'It wasn't me. It was Angel.'

'What are we going to do now?' Nick asked. 'That crazy doctor didn't seem the type to give up and she wants you and

Angel really bad. We can't count on fear of getting burned keeping her away forever. And what if she gets her hands on the other signed copies of the paperwork? Yours and Angel's commitment papers are legal documents, so Joyce and Bill would have a copy.'

I shook my head. 'I can't see Dr Wood taking the risk. Not after what she's done. She tortured Angel and me, and I'm sure we're not the only ones. We'll need to find a way to help those still trapped there. If Dr Wood so much as looks in our direction we go straight to the police, and tell them everything. From what Angel told me about what goes on in that place, it would get shut down immediately and Dr Wood's reputation would be ruined.'

Daniel frowned. 'She told you? How?'

'I hear her words in my head, as I always have. She may be mute, but she has a voice, a strong one.'

'You're incredible,' said Nick, his voice husky.

'Angel is incredible,' I said, shaking my head. 'I'm just the sidekick.'

'She would still be locked away if it wasn't for you. You are definitely not a sidekick. You're the hero.'

'If you two are going to kiss again, I'm out of here,' said Daniel before he suited his actions to his words.

I never took my eyes off Nick, marvelling at how much my life had changed since he'd offered me a lift the day before.

He believed in me, had never doubted. From the first crazy moment to now, he'd supported me. Thanks to him, I had my twin sister back and a chance to live a normal life, free of nightmares and full of possibilities.

As his lips covered mine I knew I was ready to embrace the future, and everything it offered.

Book Two

Wild Lightning

1

A ripple of energy washed over me, calling for me to leave the darkness that was my haven. I resisted, wanting to remain in blissful oblivion. The energy wave grew stronger, battering my senses, flooding every inch of my body. My skin tingled, the hairs on my arms reacting to the current coursing through me.

An image appeared in the darkness, a beautiful young woman with expressive indigo eyes and long, dark blonde hair. A single word accompanied her image, singing in the air around her.

Angel.

Her name echoed inside my head, getting louder and louder.

It stopped suddenly, the current of energy vanishing with it. My vision cleared, no longer cloaked by darkness, consciousness returning.

I sat in an overstuffed armchair, hunched over, hands curled into fists on my lap. My eyes were open, head bowed, and I frowned as I caught sight of pink fluffy slippers with grey and white cat faces on the top. I shuffled my feet, watching as the whiskers on the cats moved.

My feet.

My slippers.

I didn't recognise either of them.

I straightened up, grimacing as my body protested the move. My muscles were wound tight, stiff. How long had I been sitting like that?

I focused on my hands, working to unclench the fingers,

flexing them.

Open. Close.

Open. Close.

The white material covering my thighs bunched up with each movement. It was a nightgown, long and soft, covering me from neck to ankle. A white robe made of a sturdier weave was over the top, short sleeves leaving my arms bare from the elbows down. A thick braid of flame-coloured hair, streaked through with blonde, fell forward over my left shoulder. I reached up and tugged on the end, feeling the pull in my scalp.

It was my hair, but as unfamiliar to me as what I was wearing.

A commotion nearby caught my attention, cutting short the inspection of my appearance. I lifted my head and looked for the source of the raised voices.

Two young men stood below a television mounted on a wall to the right of me. A football game was on, and they were calling out support for their team. Both wore white pyjamas. One of them had on a robe like mine.

I heard more voices, quieter ones, and movement behind me, and twisted to find more young people spread around a large room. All wore either white nightgowns or pyjamas. It seemed to be a kind of common room, with games tables and chairs spread throughout for reading and relaxing. With everyone wearing pyjamas, it didn't appear to be a student dormitory.

Was it a hospital?

Had I been injured?

Is that why I felt like a stranger in my own body?

'Angel.'

Questions forgotten at the sound of the vision's name, I looked over to where a group of my fellow patients huddled around two newcomers. I couldn't see them clearly and tried

120

to stand, to see them better, but my muscles refused to obey.

I wanted, needed to see.

Frustration had me clenching my teeth, a curse tumbling from my lips.

The crowd of patients parted, allowing two identical young women to race through the middle of the room. I stared at them, focusing on the one wearing a long white nightgown.

Angel.

She was real.

I had to get to her.

I struggled to get out of my seat, to launch myself across the room, but all my legs did was tremble with the strain. I swayed, falling sideways against the arm of the chair, exhausted, unable to right myself.

'Easy there.' One of the young men who had been watching the game of football, the one wearing the robe, stood in front of me. He reached out and grabbed my shoulders, propping me up.

'Don't touch me,' I said, voice scratchy, throat dry.

'Holy shit.' He bounded backwards, eyes wide as he stared at me. 'Ethan, get over here. Celeste just talked.'

Celeste?

Was that my name?

I closed my eyes and sounded out the word in my head, finding nothing to connect it to. If I was Celeste, the name held no meaning for me.

'Yeah, real funny. That girl is so far gone, she's never coming back.'

'I'm telling you, Ethan, she spoke. Told me not to touch her.'

I opened my eyes to see the other guy had joined his friend, a sceptical look in his light green eyes. 'Impossible. She hasn't said a word in the entire time I've been here.'

'She's been out of it since I got here, too. One of the other

121

patients told me something went wrong with her treatment, that it fried her brain,' said the first guy.

His words set off a flood of images and sensations in my head. I was pinned down, unable to move, pain ripping through me. My screams were stifled by a gag as an older, brown-haired woman wearing a white lab coat leaned over me. She watched dispassionately as an electrical current surged through my body again and again.

I gasped, shaking my head to clear the memories and the echo of the pain they brought with them. I had to get away. Had to find Angel. I held her image in my head, whispering her name repeatedly.

'Shit, man. Did you see that? She really is awake.' The one called Ethan leaned forward. 'Hang in there, Celeste. We'll get a nurse. You're going to be fine.'

He grabbed my hand to give it a reassuring squeeze.

The second his hand touched mine the wild energy I had first felt on becoming aware surged through my body once more, slamming into his. He gasped, gripping my hand tightly. He fell to his knees in front of me, brown and gold streaks appearing in his green eyes. His body shook, the ground beneath my chair shaking with him. After what felt like an eternity he let go of my hand, eyes reverting to their original colour, and the shakes subsided. He dropped to the ground, body twitching, eyes rolling back in his head.

'What the hell did you do to him? Celeste? What did you do to Ethan?' The other guy knelt beside his friend, staring up at me with horror in his eyes.

I shook my head, unable to provide answers when I didn't know what the hell was going on. All I knew was the urge to find Angel had grown even stronger. My paralysis had vanished along with the surge of wild energy. I felt sorry for Ethan, hoped whatever I'd done hadn't hurt him permanently, but couldn't stick around to find out.

I struggled to my feet and staggered in the direction Angel and her identical twin had gone. The other patients scattered from my path, eyes wild and shocked.

Legs shaking, I stumbled down a short corridor, coming to a closed grey door. I twisted the handle, cursing when I found it locked with no sign of a keyhole. I banged on the door, shouting for someone to let me out, sensing the other patients crowding at my back. A loud murmur came from them, but I couldn't focus on individual words, as all my concentration centred on getting through this door.

The door didn't open, and there was no indication given to say if anyone on the other side had even heard me. I rattled the handle some more, but it was useless. The sense of the people behind me intensified, the murmur of words becoming a torrent, hemming me in until I wanted to scream at them to go away, to leave me alone.

A keypad was beside the door, level with the handle. I jabbed the buttons, not caring which numbers I pushed, just needing it to open. Tears spilled down my cheeks when it flashed an error message at me.

I could no longer hold in my screams.

The crowd of people behind me shuffled back, but I had no time to worry about them.

Pressure was building up behind my eyes, skin tingling and the hairs on my arms rising. I felt a current, different from whatever it was that had hit Ethan, flow through my body towards the hand touching the keypad. Sparks flew from my fingertips, spearing into the unit.

I heard a sizzling noise inside the keypad a second before the display lit up and the lock disengaged. I yanked on the handle, wrenching the door open and scurrying through as fast as my trembling legs could carry me. I entered a large reception area filled with minimal furniture. A young woman bolted up from behind a circular front desk to stand in my path.

'Stop right there.' She put both hands up in front of her, sidestepping to stay in front of me when I tried to go around her.

'Oh no you don't. Dr Wood will kill me if I let another one of you escape,' she said as she reached out and grabbed hold of my arm, digging her nails in.

The mention of Dr Wood flooded my head with images of being pinned down again, along with the remembered agony coursing through my body. I screamed, feeling a surge of energy rush through me. Twin bolts of lightning shot out of my hands, knocking the woman back. She fell backwards and then scrambled away from me on her hands and knees, head down, as more bolts shot every which way, connecting with the walls, floor and ceiling.

Louds pops sounded as one by one all the lights went out, the gentle hum of the computers behind the front desk dying along with them. Seconds later, an alarm shrieked deep within the building.

Sunshine streamed in through large windows on either side of the front foyer. The receptionist made no move to stop me as I ran over to the sliding doors set between them.

The doors didn't open at my approach and I skidded to a stop, prying at the gap between them with my fingers, ignoring the pain it caused. It was hopeless. I was too weak to force the doors apart. I scanned the wall on either side of the doors, looking for an emergency release. There had to be one, in case of a power blackout.

There.

A red button to the left of the door. I pushed it, gulping down relief as the doors slowly slid open. I darted through as soon as there was a big enough gap and tore off down the front stairs. I hit a wide concrete area with car parks on either side. Blood pounding, I ran through the middle, heading for the driveway leading out, breath hissing in my ears, legs trembling with each step. I felt so weak, drained of energy, but I couldn't afford to stop.

I had to find Angel.

Only then would I be safe.

I didn't question how I knew she was the answer to everything. I felt it in every part of me.

Once I found her, and touched her, the nightmare would end.

I reached the end of a long winding driveway and stepped through an open set of large wrought iron gates hanging from wide brick columns. Both columns bore plaques that read Wood Estate. A shudder rippled through my body at the sight of them, and I averted my eyes as I hurried past. I never doubted I was going in the right direction, the soft slap of my slippers the only sound other than my harsh breathing as I ran.

Soon another sound penetrated my single-minded focus. Car engine. There was no sign of the approaching vehicle, but it wouldn't be long before it rounded the bend I could see up the road. When it did, the occupants would see me instantly. I stopped running and eyed the grass lining the ditch on the closest side of the road. Dressed as I was, one look at me would be sure to arouse suspicion. I threw myself into the ditch beside the road, lying as flat and still as I could, hoping the tall grass would be enough to hide me from a casual glance.

I heard a vehicle drive by. I waited for a long moment, wanting to make sure the occupants were far from sight before I rose. I lifted on my elbows, preparing to get up, only to freeze when the sound of another engine reached me.

I flopped to the ground, ignoring the grass stalks brushing my face, and the feel of the hard earth beneath my body as I lay there. A long moment passed before I pushed myself up to my elbows once more. My muscles ached, quivering as I forced myself to my feet. Earlier momentum lost, I could barely manage a fast walk as I once again stumbled off in search of Angel.

No matter how long it took, I would find her.

2

Exhausted, throat so dry it hurt to swallow, I stumbled up the driveway of a lowset block of units, eyes fixed on the doorway to the left. Angel was somewhere behind that door. The invisible path I'd followed for the last several hours had guided me unerringly to this point.

The sun had been high in the sky when I'd first started out, the shadows of early evening appearing as I trudged the last couple of blocks. I'd tossed my white robe in a backyard soon after hitting the town outskirts, slipping through an open gate to steal a flowing black dress off the clothesline and throwing it on over the nightgown. I couldn't do anything about my slippers, but the dress had proved enough of a disguise to get me here without any fuss.

I reached the front door of the unit and raised my hand to knock, head hanging low. Each breath felt as if my lungs were filled with jagged shards of glass, weariness closing my eyes no matter how hard I fought to keep them open.

I rested my head upon the closed door, tumbling forward when it opened. Strong arms wrapped around me, stopping me from falling to the ground. I forced my eyes open and looked up into the worried indigo eyes of a good looking young man with light brown hair. He gave me a reassuring smile as he scooped me up in his arms, calling out for someone inside the unit to come and help him.

He hugged me against his body, murmuring words of reassurance, the fresh clean scent of him wrapping around me as he carried me inside the unit. For the first time since I had come to in the Wood Estate, I knew I was safe.

Safe in the arms of a stranger.

I felt myself being carried a short distance before I was laid down on a soft surface and a pillow placed under my head. The scent enveloping me was the same as that of my rescuer. I closed my eyes and relaxed into the bed, allowing the tension in my body to fade.

I could feel him there, standing beside the bed, his bed, watching over me. I wanted to smile and thank him for his kindness, but the journey to get to this point had sapped all my energy. I was helpless to do anything but lie there, my breathing easing as my body sought to recover from the punishment I had put it through.

A moment later I heard the soft murmur of voices and strained to catch their meaning.

'Where did she come from?' This was a female's voice.

'She was just there, when I opened the door. Practically fell into my arms.' My rescuer's voice was low, deep, threaded through with worry. 'Should we call the police? An ambulance?'

I struggled to force out a denial. I had to make them understand.

'Angel,' I whispered, the name barely audible to my own ears. I tried again, putting every ounce of energy I could muster into making myself heard.

'Angel.'

'What the hell?' This was the female again. 'She just said Angel.' Cool hands touched my cheeks, turning my head. 'Who are you? How do you know Angel?'

'Andie, careful. You'll hurt her.'

'Daniel, you heard her say Angel's name, same as I did. We need to know who she is. What if this is a trap? We have to know.'

Despite the urgency behind her words, the hands touching me were gentle as they probed my neck, checking my pulse

128

before prying my eyelids open. I wanted to reassure her, to tell her I was no threat to Angel, but the lethargy that had swept over me would not let up.

Then she touched my forehead.

A light flared behind my eyes and I felt a build-up of pressure inside my head. I moaned, not wanting to do to her whatever it was I had done to Ethan. But instead of a wild flare of energy sweeping from my body to hers, warmth radiated from her touch. The warmth travelled throughout my body, sweeping away my lethargy, making my weakened muscles tingle. It left me feeling renewed, revitalised, and I never wanted it to end. I frowned when she removed her hands and the flood of whatever it was she was pouring into me stopped.

It took a moment for me to realise the sense of well-being generated by her touch remained, giving me the strength to open my eyes. I blinked several times to clear my vision as I looked into a face identical to Angel's. But even without the young man, Daniel, calling her Andie, I would have known she was not the one I sought.

The pull that had led me here did not connect to the young woman standing in front of me. She was the twin I had glimpsed as she and Angel ran through the common room, back at the estate.

Andie wore a stunned expression as she backed away from me. Daniel, confusion evident in his gaze, looked from her to me and back again. He was tall, at least thirty centimetres taller than Andie. While his hair was brown instead of dark blonde, the similarity of their indigo eyes suggested they were related.

She clutched his arm. 'Daniel. This girl, she's like Angel.'

Daniel's eyes went wide as he stared at me. 'Are you sure?'

'I could feel her, here, when I was touching her.' Andie

tapped the side of her head. 'I'm not one hundred percent sure how I did it, but I think I gave her some of my energy, made her stronger, the way I did for Angel.'

'You think she's another one of Dr Wood's experiments?'

I didn't hear Andie's response, the mention of Dr Wood triggering another of the excruciatingly vivid waking nightmares. I whimpered, scrambling to a sitting position, wrapping my arms around my torso. I rocked backward and forwards, eyes clamped shut as I sought to ward off the terrifying images and memories of pain.

'Hey, hey, it's okay. You're safe. She can't hurt you anymore.' I felt the mattress shift as Daniel sat beside me.

He took me in his arms, rubbing his hands over my back as he continued to murmur words of comfort and reassurance. I let his touch and the sound of his voice soothe me, letting out a shuddering sigh as the memories began to release their grip on me. When I was sure I wasn't going to be sucked under by the maelstrom of memories, I reluctantly pulled away from him.

His hands lingered on my arms for a moment before he let go and scooted further down the bed to give me space. His beautiful indigo eyes remained focused on mine, and I found strength in his steady regard. I released another sigh and relaxed back against the headboard.

'Well, I guess that answers the question of where she came from,' said Andie. She stood beside the bed, arms crossed in front of her chest, a frown creasing her brow. 'But it doesn't explain who she is or how she got here.'

She looked towards the open door behind her. 'What if they sent her here, like a Trojan Horse, to confuse us? They could be out there right now, preparing to storm the place and take Angel away from us again.' Her voice rose, and she took a step towards the door.

'No one sent me,' I said, voice raspy. The dryness of my

throat made me wince, but I forced myself to keep talking, hoping she could read the truth in my eyes. 'I escaped just after you and Angel did. I ran after you, but you were–'

A hacking cough forced its way out of my lungs, doubling me over. I coughed and coughed, dimly aware of Daniel rubbing my back again.

'Here, drink this,' said Andie. She placed a bottle of water into my hand. 'Sip it slowly, and you'll be okay.'

I gratefully gulped down a few small mouthfuls, trying not to guzzle the entire bottle in one go as the water worked its magic on my inflamed throat.

Reflex coughs, like aftershocks, tickled my chest as I lowered the bottle and clutched it in both hands. After a moment the aftershocks also subsided and I could breathe a little more easily. I looked around the room, Daniel's bedroom. Other than a built-in wardrobe, a dresser and the bed I was currently sitting on, there wasn't much to see.

There was nothing to tell me what kind of person he was. But his treatment of me had already told me enough.

He'd taken me in without hesitation, and offered me reassurance and comfort just as easily. I'd instinctively known I was safe with him, from the first moment he took me in his arms. Every action since then told me I was right to trust him, to feel safe in his presence. I looked over at Andie, unable to miss the wary expression on her face or the rigid way she held herself. But, like her brother, her actions gave away her kind heart.

I was safe here. I could tell them the truth.

'My name is Celeste, I think,' I said, giving them a rueful smile. 'At least, that's what two guys back at that place called me.' Even though I didn't name it, I still shuddered. I had to get over it; couldn't afford to lose it again.

I focused on Daniel's eyes, using his steady gaze to anchor myself to the here and now.

'You don't know your own name? How is that possible?' Andie took a step closer to the bed, pulling my gaze from her brother.

Her eyes, so like his, were narrowed. I didn't blame her for being suspicious. I'd be wary of someone showing up on my doorstep, asking for help, claiming not to know who they were. But it was the truth, and I hoped she could see that.

'I don't know. I don't remember anything from before I woke up.' I shrugged. 'That's not even the right word. I think I was always awake, I just wasn't aware. It was like drifting in the dark, my mind shut down, and then I felt this massive wave of energy.'

I'd felt safe in the dark, hidden where no one could find me. The living nightmares I'd been experiencing gave a hint of what it was I was hiding from, and whom.

But not why.

The vision of Angel had drawn me from that place. I hoped she would be able to provide answers to the questions clamouring away inside of me. But for her to free the rest of me from the dark recesses of my mind, I needed Andie to let me see her, touch her. I had to convince her to help me, make her see how important it was, that everything revolved around my getting to Angel.

'I saw Angel in here.' I tapped my head. 'Heard her name. The sound of it pulled me out of the darkness, triggering a return to consciousness. I found myself sitting in a chair in the middle of a large room, surrounded by young people wearing pyjamas. I figured it must have been a hospital, and I'd been injured. Then I saw Angel, for real this time, as the two of you ran through the room. I knew I had to follow you, to get to Angel. I knew once I was with her everything would make sense.'

I bit my bottom lip, suddenly fighting back tears as I switched my gaze to Daniel. 'I know she's here. I can sense her. I need to see her. I need to know what's wrong with me. If I can just touch her everything will be okay.'

Tears spilled down my cheeks. 'Please help me.'

'It's okay. We'll help you, Celeste.' He leaned forward and gently brushed my tears away with his thumb. I leaned into his touch, liking the way he said my name. For the first time since I'd heard it, I felt it belonged to me.

'Hang on a minute. How do we even know she's telling the truth?'

Daniel removed his hand from my cheek, leaving me feeling oddly bereft, and frowned at Andie. 'Look at her. Does she look as if she's lying? She's terrified, alone, desperate. She needs us, just like Angel did. We must help her. You said it yourself, this afternoon. We need to do something about the others the crazy doctor has locked up. Well, Celeste is one of them.'

Andie shook her head, and I caught the gleam of unshed tears in her luminous eyes. 'I know. I know. But, we just got Angel back. She's still so weak. They tortured her, Daniel, over and over again. What if helping Celeste sets back her recovery? And they're bound to come after us. We cannot let Angel fall back into Dr Wood's hands.'

'We won't. We'll keep them both safe, Angel and Celeste.'

Daniel's assurance echoed in my head, and I clung to it to ward off the nightmare induced by Andie's mention of Dr Wood. My hands twitched, dropping the water bottle, fingernails digging into my palms. My breath came in gasps as I fought to remain in control. I would not lose it; could not afford to lose it. Not if I wanted them to help me.

'We'll make sure Dr Wood never hurts either of them again,' said Daniel.

I lost my grip on what little sanity I had left when an avalanche of pain-filled memories swept over me. Strapped to a table, gag in my mouth to silence my screams, lights blinding me. The woman in the white lab coat, expression one of cool detachment, flicking the switch to send agonising jolts of electricity into my body. Body arching, heels drumming the table, jaw clenching, the taste of blood in my mouth.

I could feel it now, body locking up as a current raced through it, begging for release.

Daniel moved to touch me, and I screamed at him to get away as I launched myself off the bed. I bolted to the corner of the room farthest away from him, huddling between the dresser and the wall on the opposite side.

The build-up of energy inside me intensified. Hands still clenched into fists, I could feel sparks shooting from my fingertips and into my palms. It didn't hurt me, passing harmlessly into my flesh, but I instinctively knew it would be a different matter for another person.

I had to contain it.

I kept my eyes open, focused on Daniel's alarmed expression, shaking my head when it looked as if he was going to approach.

Andie took his arm and pulled him across the room, talking to him the whole time. I couldn't hear a word she said, my ears filled with the crackle of current. It was getting stronger, louder.

I couldn't hold it.

I had to let it go.

I kept my hands clenched as I raised them towards the ceiling, blue sparks lighting them up from within. I sucked in a deep breath and let out one last scream as I opened my hands and let the energy go.

Lightning bolts slammed into the ceiling, sending a shower of sparks around the room. The bulb inside the light fixture in the middle of the ceiling shattered, glass falling to the floor in an explosive cascade. Shadows coated the room, moonlight streaming in through the window allowing me to see matching expressions of horror on Daniel and Andie's faces.

They were right to be horrified. I had to be a monster to be able to do what I just did.

Maybe that was why I was at that place, being tortured? Because I was a monster, they were trying to cure, to stop me hurting people the way I had hurt Ethan.

'You're not a monster. You're just different. Like me.'

The voice sounded like Andie's, but I knew it didn't belong to her.

I looked over to the doorway of the room to where Angel stood, form backlit by a light in the hallway. She wore the same kind of white nightgown as the one I had on under the black dress I'd stolen.

She wore a gentle smile, no trace of condemnation or fear on her face as she walked toward me, carefully skirting the broken glass on the floor.

I smiled back at her, conscious of the tears streaking my face. Everything was going to be okay now.

Angel was here.

I'd found her.

I stretched out my hand to touch hers.

3

'Angel, no.' Andie raced forward and pulled her away from me. 'Don't touch her.'

'It's okay,' said Angel, patting her sister on the arm. 'She won't hurt me. I'll be fine,'

I shook my head. 'She's right. I would never hurt her.'

Andie's mouth gaped open as she stared at me. 'You heard her?'

I frowned. 'Of course. I may have lost my memory, but I'm not deaf. My ears work just fine.'

'No. You don't understand. Angel is mute. I'm the only one that can hear her.' Andie tapped the side of her head. 'In here.' Then she grimaced. 'Well, I used to be the only one who could hear her.'

Angel placed a hand on Andie's shoulder, mouth not moving as she said, 'I don't know why she can hear me, but I'm glad. After fifteen years without anyone being able to hear me, it is wonderful to have someone else I can talk to besides you.'

'Oh, I didn't mean it like that.' Andie hugged Angel. 'I'm glad she can hear you, too. I wish everyone could hear you. You might never have been sent to the Wood Estate if that were the case.'

I gritted my teeth against the onslaught of memories and the strange flow of energy sure to follow the naming of the place where I had been tortured.

Angel hurried over to me, hands outstretched. I clutched them, sparks flaring at the first touch. She gripped my hands tightly and I flinched, half expecting a repeat of when I'd shattered the lightbulb or the crazy flare of energy that had knocked Ethan unconscious. Instead, my hands tingled like pins and needles but somehow better, refreshing. The sensation quickly spread until every inch of my body zinged, the pale blonde hairs on my arms standing up.

Light spilled from between our joined hands as we faced one another. It flared around us, washing away the shadows in the room. I caught sight of Daniel in my peripheral vision, his eyes wide and amazed as he stared at us. I felt the same kind of wonder. This was nothing like what had happened to Ethan. Then the energy had exploded out of my body, slamming into his.

With Angel, we were sharing energy. It pulsed between us, gentle and soothing. I lost track of time as we stood there. Finally, the sensation faded, the light dying with it, and we were once again standing in shadows.

I blinked, eyes adjusting to the change, and let go of Angel's hands. I stepped back and closed my eyes, focusing on my sense of self, ready to discover who I truly was.

My shoulders sagged when all I found was a blank slate.

With my single-minded drive to get to Angel, I'd thought, hoped, that seeing her, making contact, would trigger my memories. I'd finally know who I was and what had happened to me.

But nothing had changed.

'Let's move into the lounge,' said Andie. 'At least that way we'll be able to see each other better while we try to figure out what the hell is going on here. It's been a crazy weekend, but whatever just happened is crazier still.'

'Crazier than finding out you had an identical twin sister, were told she died fifteen years ago, only to find she was very much alive, held prisoner by an evil doctor, and was waiting for you to come rescue her?' Angel wore a rueful smile as her voice sounded in my head.

'Crazier than that,' said Andie over her shoulder as she led the way out of the room. 'I'm going to call Nick. I'm thinking we're going to need his help sorting all this out.'

I must have looked puzzled as Daniel immediately explained, 'Nick is my friend and workmate, and Andie's new boyfriend.' His smile was tight, tone clipped, eyebrows arching.

'Oh,' I said, at a loss for anything else to say. Clearly, Andie's choice of boyfriend was a sore point for Daniel. But Andie didn't seem to pay any attention to her brother's mild grumble as she scooped a mobile phone off the coffee table in the middle of the lounge room and moved into a small kitchen area to call Nick.

Daniel gestured for me to take a seat on the couch, sitting beside me once I'd done so. Angel sat in an armchair on the left, tucking her feet up as she stared expectantly at me. I didn't know what it was she was waiting for, and resisted the urge to fidget, searching for something to say to break the silence filling the room.

Before I could speak, Andie rushed back into the room, phone held in one hand. 'Nick will be over soon, but he said we need to turn the television on, right now. There's a news report about Celeste on Channel 8.'

I froze as Daniel picked up a remote and pointed it at the television, selecting the correct channel. The words "Breaking News" scrolled across the bottom of the screen as a female journalist with a microphone in one hand, and a serious expression on her perfectly made up face, stood in front of a senior police officer.

'Do the police suspect foul play is involved in the disappearance of the young woman?'

The police officer's face was sombre as he said, 'At this point we do not have any concrete evidence to suggest anyone else was involved in the young woman's disappearance.

According to staff at the care facility, she had been in a catatonic state for two months and has just woken up and wandered off. She is presumably confused and disoriented, and they urgently request anyone with information about her whereabouts to call us as she's in need of immediate medical treatment.'

'Can you share more information about the young woman, a recent photo, so people know who to look out for?'

'I'm afraid, due to the nature of the care she has been receiving, we are unable to provide a photograph or any personal details. But we do have a description. She is nineteen years old, approximately 160cm tall with a slender build. She has red hair, hazel eyes and a pale complexion, and was last seen wearing a long white nightgown and pink slippers.'

The police officer looked directly at the camera. 'If anyone has seen this young woman, it is imperative they get in touch with the Easton Police Department, so we can locate her and ensure she receives the urgent medical treatment she needs.'

He seemed about to say something else, but the journalist turned to face the camera, microphone held up to her own lips. 'Please, if you have seen this young woman, or know where she might be, let the Easton Police know so she can be returned to those who love and care for her.'

I sagged back against the couch when the view shifted to the anchors back at the newsroom as they reiterated the plea to the public for assistance in finding me. For a moment, I'd thought the police officer was going to answer so many of the questions filling my head. Instead I'd learned how old I was, and physical details I could find out myself by looking in a mirror.

And that I'd been catatonic.

Still, I felt no relief in having a name for the darkness I had taken shelter in. I turned to face Angel. She was the reason I'd regained my senses. I opened my mouth, not sure if I wanted to thank her or berate her for the part she'd played in my awakening.

She spoke before I could get a word out.

'You're like me,' she said. 'Is that why you were there, so they could experiment on your powers? I lived at the estate for fifteen years, and until six months ago I was kept upstairs with the rest of the patients. I've never seen you before, so you must have arrived after I was imprisoned in the lowest level. I was only allowed out at night, for exercise, to prevent me from escaping again, and I never realised they were holding anyone else like me prisoner.' She frowned. 'They can't have been, or Dr ... she would have said something. She would have put us together for sure, to see what would happen.'

Grateful for her tact in not mentioning the doctor's name, I shrugged. 'I don't know why I was there. I don't know anything.' That was the problem.

Her eyes widened. 'You have amnesia. Like when Andie forgot I even existed.'

'I guess. All I know is I woke up in that place, saw you escape, and knew I had to find you.' I lowered my eyes, remembering the mad scramble to leave the estate, the overwhelming urge to get to Angel.

Now I was here, even though I still had no memory, I felt oddly content. It was as if I'd come home, which should have felt weird as these people were complete strangers to me. Then again, I was a stranger to myself.

'Okay, you two are obviously having a conversation, but it is kind of strange to be hearing only one side of it,' said Daniel as he switched the television off again.

I faced him. 'I'm sorry. I keep forgetting you can't hear her.'

'Frustrating, isn't it,' said Andie as she perched herself on the arm of Angel's chair. 'When we were little, no one believed me when I said I could hear Angel. They all thought I was making it up, that it was just a game.'

'I thought it was a twin thing,' said Daniel. 'But unless Celeste is another long-lost twin, or triplet, I guess, if there were three of you, her being able to hear Angel blows that theory out of the water.'

My pulse pounded in my ears and I sucked in a breath at the thought of suddenly finding out I was related to the three of them. But it wasn't possible. I didn't look anything like Andie and Angel.

Did I?

The police officer said I had hazel eyes to go with the reddish blonde plait that kept falling forward over my right shoulder. But other than that, I had no idea what I looked like. Oh God.

What if I was hideous?

I ducked my head to hide the flush I could feel sweeping over my face. Crazy to be worrying about my appearance, when there were so many more important things to worry about, but now the thought had lodged in my head I couldn't block it out.

I rose, causing raised eyebrows all around. 'I need to go to the bathroom.'

'Down the hall, the door across from Daniel's room,' said Andie.

It was a conscious effort not to sprint, maintaining what dignity I could as I made my way to the bathroom and shut the door behind me. A large oval mirror hung on the wall above the vanity and I stood in front of it, staring at my reflection.

A stranger stared back at me.

She had pale skin, covered in light coloured freckles. The eyes were set above rounded cheekbones. She was pretty enough, the girl in the mirror, but her eyes looked haunted, dark smudges beneath them standing out against the paleness of her skin. I lifted a hand and placed it on my cheek, the stranger in the mirror copying the movement perfectly.

I couldn't deny she was me, but looking at my reflection prompted nothing but disappointment. No memories, not even a vague sense of having seen the face somewhere but being unable to place it.

I sighed and turned away from my reflection, not ready to return to the lounge.

A light knock at the door made me jump.

'Yes?'

'I thought you might want to have a shower, freshen up,' said Andie. 'I have some clean clothes for you. You're about the same size as me and Angel, so they should fit.'

Tears stung my eyes at this act of kindness. I keep my gaze averted as I opened the door and accepted the offered bundle with a murmur of thanks.

'There's soap, shampoo, conditioner, everything you need in the cupboard under the basin. Use whatever you want,' she said before backing away.

I closed the door and put the clothes she'd given me on top of the vanity, quickly shedding the oversized black dress I'd stolen and the white nightgown, relieved to be done with them.

Minutes later, washed, dried and dressed in a faded pair of blue jeans and a Wonder Woman T-shirt, I felt refreshed, renewed, and ready to face whatever the future might hold as I combed out the tangles in my wet hair. I had no past, but my headlong flight had brought me to kind and caring people.

With their help, I was sure everything would be okay.

4

Angel stood up when I re-entered the lounge. She held a bundle of clothes like those I was wearing and moved past me with a smile, heading for the bathroom. I heard Andie moving around in the kitchen, and the sound of a kettle boiling.

I was alone with Daniel.

Warmth flooded my cheeks, a tingle low in my belly radiating out and washing over me at his steady gaze. He leaned back on the couch, smiling encouragingly as he indicated for me to sit beside him. I perched on the edge of the seat, back straight, hands clasped in my lap.

'Andie's making us something to eat, and some coffee,' he said. 'We figure this is going to be a long night.'

I lowered my eyes, picking at the hem on my borrowed shirt. 'I'm sorry for getting you all mixed up in my problems. I was so focused on finding Angel, I didn't think about what would happen when I did. You've all been so kind. I don't want to put you out any further.'

He stretched out his hand and took hold of mine, giving it a squeeze. 'Don't worry about it. We were already neck deep in trouble anyway.'

Sincerity shone in his eyes, his hand still holding mine. His thumb stroked the back of my hand in a soothing gesture. Each slow stroke made the tingle in my stomach intensify. I should have pulled my hand away, severed the connection, but I didn't want him to think I was being rude. So, we sat there, holding hands.

Andie bustled into the room, carrying a plate loaded up with toasted ham and cheese sandwiches. I pulled my hand free of Daniel's as she deposited the plate on the coffee table before returning to the kitchen. Seconds later she was back with two cups of coffee.

She waved a hand at the coffee she set in front of me. 'I was going to ask how you like your coffee, but with you having no memory I figured there wasn't any point. So I made it with milk and two sugars. Hope it's okay. If not, I can just keep on making coffee until you find one you do like.'

'I'm sure it will be fine, thank you,' I said, smiling up at her, relieved for something else to focus on other than the strange feelings her brother inspired in me. 'You don't need to go to all that trouble for me.'

'No trouble,' she said over her shoulder as she headed back to the kitchen, soon returning with two more coffees.

Angel exited the bathroom, dressed in jeans and a pink T-shirt with a grey and white cat on the front, her long hair wet and loose like mine. She scooped up a sandwich on her way through the lounge before sitting back in the armchair.

'Maybe I should have given you that shirt, Celeste,' said Andie with a laugh. 'It would have matched your slippers.' She picked up a sandwich and sat on the other side of me, making me slide closer to Daniel.

'This shirt is fine,' I said, trying to straighten up, conscious of Daniel's long leg pressing against mine. I could feel the warmth of it through my jeans. I cleared my throat as I shifted to face Andie. 'I promise, I'll give you your clothes back as soon as I can.'

'Hey, don't sweat it. I live in jeans and shirts. I've got plenty to spare.'

'She's not kidding,' said Daniel. 'She has dozens of the things, in every colour you can think of. Can't remember the last time I saw Andie in a dress or a skirt.' He leaned forward and picked up the plate of sandwiches, holding it up in front of me.

I had no appetite, but I took one just to have something to do with my hands. I nibbled on my sandwich, struggling to focus on Andie's next words.

'After being forced to dress like a lady for fifteen years, I never want to wear a dress or a skirt again,' Andie said, as she reached out to grab another sandwich before Daniel put the plate back on the coffee table.

Daniel grabbed two sandwiches, one for each hand, and the two of them grinned at one another, the bond between them evident. Angel appeared equally at ease as she munched on her sandwich and sipped coffee. I rested my sandwich on my lap and reached out to pick up the coffee cup. I took a cautious sip, pleased to find I liked the taste.

Add one more item to the list of what I knew about myself. I liked my coffee white with two sugars.

A brief smile curved my lips, and then died as I thought about all the stuff I still didn't know.

Did I have a brother or a sister somewhere, wondering where I was? Or a boyfriend? Somewhere, was there a guy like Daniel waiting for me to come home? Maybe that was why I felt so comfortable in his presence, because he reminded me of someone from my forgotten past?

Until my memory returned, I had no way of knowing who I was or who might be looking for me.

From what I'd heard earlier, Angel had been separated from her siblings, locked away in that awful place, for fifteen years. What if I'd been missing for that long as well? My family could be out there now, desperately searching for me. Maybe they'd see the news report and realise I was the missing girl from the description. Perhaps it would be best if I went to the police station and turned myself in so they could come find me, and take me home.

Then again, what if they'd been told I was dead?

It was all so confusing. I didn't know what the right thing

to do was. Had no experience to guide me. My thoughts were going round and round in circles, always coming back to the same thing,

I had a blank wall where my memories should be. I knew my first name, and how I liked my coffee, but nothing else, except that when I was upset or scared I could shoot lightning out of my fingers. Amnesia or not, I knew normal people couldn't do that.

I put my mug back on the coffee table, working hard to swallow the lump in my throat as I asked, 'What am I? What did those people do to me, to make me this way?'

Silence met my questions at first, and then Daniel moved closer, once again taking my hand in his. 'We'll help you figure it out. Somehow, we'll figure it out.'

I clung to his hand, eyes fixed on his, and the lifeline he represented. I needed his touch, his surety everything was going to be okay. Not that I thought it was going to be as simple as his confidence suggested.

'What do you remember?' Andie asked.

Focusing on the feel of Daniel's hand in mine, on the strength and decency I could sense in him, I told them everything. If my voice shook as I described what I saw when the waking nightmares hit they didn't comment. As I talked, Daniel continued to stroke the back of my hand, giving it a squeeze when I faltered in my retelling.

Tears stung my eyes when I felt a soft fluttering sensation inside my head.

Warmth and acceptance flowed along with it, and I looked over to see Angel smiling gently at me. She'd suffered the same as I had, and yet still had the compassion and grace to reach out to let me know I wasn't alone. I took a deep breath, and continued with the details of my escape.

'How the hell can anyone consider electric shock to be a form of therapy,' said Daniel, when I had finished, gripping my hand tight. 'That's insane. Nick and I work with electricity all the time, and there is nothing therapeutic in getting hit by stray volts.'

I managed a small smile at this sign of outrage on my behalf as I said, 'So, now you know everything I do. No memory. No last name. And a crazy ability to shatter lightbulbs with lightning and knock people out.' My hand shook as I once again picked up the coffee Andie had made for me.

'Well, as far as crazy abilities go, that's pretty cool. Angel can set fires, manipulate objects with her mind, and sometimes see events before they happen. Andie is a reservoir for power that Angel can tap into to make her abilities stronger and to heal. It clearly also worked on you. As for me, I'm just an ordinary guy. Nothing special about me.'

I put the coffee cup down, wanting to protest, to tell him how special he was. His kindness, his willingness to take in a stranger, offering unconditional support and assistance without question; they were truly amazing qualities. But I knew if I tried to tell him how I saw him, I would trip over the words and make a fool of myself.

'People saw what you did, when you escaped. They're sure to tell the doctor, and she's going to come looking for you. You and Angel are what she needs to prove her theory about people with psychic abilities to her former colleagues.' Andie's voice was solemn as she gazed from her sister to me.

She stood up. 'As soon as Nick arrives, we need to leave. Find somewhere safe where we can figure out what to do next.'

Daniel let go of my hand and got up, moving over to the front window. 'You called Nick over half an hour ago. He should have been here by now.' He peered out into the street.

'Shit.' He spun around, body tense. 'There's a police car out there.' He vaulted the coffee table and took my hand, giving me no time to think as he pulled me to my feet. 'We have to get out of here.' He dragged me through the kitchen, toward a back door, with Andie and Angel on our heels.

A loud knock sounded on the front door, the sound stealing my breath. I willed Daniel to go faster. We had to get away.

'Wait,' said Angel.

'Angel said to wait,' said Andie.

Daniel paused with his hand on the doorknob. I felt the tension radiating from him. Angel moved to stand beside him, placing her hand on the door itself, eyes closed. A moment later she opened them.

'It's clear,' she said. 'But more police are on their way. We need to go left once we get through the back-neighbour's yard. Then we must take the first street on the right.'

Andie relayed Angel's words to Daniel. He wasted no time wrenching open the back door and pulling me out into the backyard.

5

What little composure I had gained during the brief time I'd been with Daniel, Andie and Angel vanished as we fled into the night. I felt the build-up of energy inside me, and the thought of being captured and returned to where I had been tortured was beyond terrifying. I fought to hold on, to not let the memories overwhelm me again. The last thing we needed was for me to freak out and signal to every police officer in the area where we were by an explosion of lightning.

I hadn't put my slippers back on after my shower, and the grass beneath my feet was cool and wet from dew. I focused on the chilling sensation, digging my toes in with each stride as the four of us ran to the back fence, dodging a clothesline and a small outdoor setting under a large tree.

The fence was waist high, made of a thick metal mesh, and Daniel steadied me as I clambered over it. He did the same for his sisters and then vaulted it easily, landing lightly beside me. He took my hand again as we weaved through the backyard we had taken refuge in, dodging children's play equipment as we went.

Upbeat music sounded close by, startling a scream from between my clenched lips.

'Shit,' said Andie, as she pressed against the side of a large wooden cubby house and fished a mobile phone out of the back pocket of her jeans. She frantically pressed the screen as the music got louder. We crowded around her, eyes on the light shining from the device as she held it up to her ear.

'Nick,' she whispered hoarsely into the phone. 'Don't

come to the flat. The police are after us. Don't go home either, in case they are after you too. We're on our way to McLellen Street. Meet us there.' She didn't give him time to answer, hanging up and stashing the phone away again, nervously looking over her shoulder.

'Do you think they heard that?' She swivelled to face Angel.

Angel closed her eyes. 'They're still at the front door. They are calling for us to come outside, and getting ready to break the door down if we don't respond.' She opened her eyes and looked at me. 'They're looking for Celeste. You were spotted by a couple of people on your way to us.'

Andie told Daniel what Angel had said, and his grip on my hand tightened.

I swallowed heavily before I said, 'If it's just me they want, maybe I should hand myself in. I don't want to get you all in trouble with the police.' Maybe they wouldn't take me back to the estate. Maybe the police would reunite me with my family.

If I had one.

If they wanted me back.

For all I knew it could have been my family that had sent me to the estate in the first place, because of what I could do. I wanted to take back my offer to hand myself in to the police, but the words couldn't be unsaid. Breath held, I waited for the others to decide if they wanted to get rid of me or not.

'You are not turning yourself in,' said Daniel. 'It's too dangerous.'

'He's right. If the police get their hands on you, they'll have no choice but to take you back to the estate,' said Andie. 'Once they do, you can guarantee the doctor will never give you another chance to escape.'

Relief nearly sapped the strength from my legs. I didn't protest as Daniel tugged me along with him, Angel and Andie right behind us. We hurried down the side of the house and then raced down the driveway.

I squeaked when a large dog charged toward the fence of the neighbouring house. It let out a deep bark, the sound carrying in the still night. It continued to bark, getting louder and more frenzied as we ran by. A chorus of barks sounded in nearby yards as more dogs joined in.

We turned left, as Angel had said we should, and darted across the road to take the first corner on the right. I looked up at the street sign as we ran toward it, moonlight allowing me to read "McLellen Street".

The bitumen beneath was nowhere near as forgiving as the grass had been, but I forced myself to keep up the pace despite the rough surface beneath my feet, gritting my teeth to prevent a cry each time I stepped on a rock. My companions were equally silent, and I couldn't remember if any of them had been wearing shoes or not.

I was grateful for the burst of energy, or whatever it had been, that had flowed into my body when I'd been touched by Andie and then Angel. Without it my legs would have collapsed long ago, the muscles weakened by however long I had been catatonic for. From what Ethan and his friend had said, I'd been like that for several weeks at least.

Thinking of Ethan brought back the horror of what I'd done, the power bursting out of me and striking him down. I pushed the memory away as we rounded the corner, crying out when headlights flared, blinding me. A car was stopped in the middle of the street in front of us and I flung up my free hand to protect my eyes, unable to prevent a gasp of dismay when red and blue lights flickered to life on the roof of the car.

I pulled on Daniel's hand, desperate to flee, but he didn't let go as he continued moving forward, giving me no choice but to follow.

Angel shouted in my head, calling for us to dodge around the police car and to jump the low fence of the house on the right.

Heart pounding, breath coming in gasps, I clutched Daniel's hand, praying Angel knew what she was doing as we followed the path she set. With Andie at her side, she led us through a rabbit warren of backyards, a cacophony of dog barks meeting us at every turn. Some of the home owners shouted for their dogs to be quiet, while others yelled in alarm to see strangers bolting through their backyards.

It wouldn't be hard for the police to track us with all the noise following in our wake. Multiple sirens sounded in the background, setting even more dogs wailing, as the police hunted us down. They weren't going to give up, relentless in their pursuit.

We darted through yards, crossed numerous streets, and I was sure we were going to be caught at any moment. Shoulders hunched forward, I waited for the outcry that said the chase was won, dreading the moment and yet wanting to get it over and done with at the same time. Then Angel called a halt, getting us to huddle together underneath a two-storey house that appeared to be empty. As my breathing slowed, I realised the sound of sirens and dogs barking had grown faint.

We'd done it.

We'd got away.

I slumped against Daniel, brushing damp hair out of my eyes, only to stiffen when I heard a car engine approaching. Angel motioned for us to stay where we were as a car drove slowly past the house under which we hid.

It was a police car, siren silenced, the lights on its roof switched off. I held my breath, sure even the slightest exhale would reveal our presence. But the car didn't stop, and soon Angel urged us into the street. The second we set foot on the bitumen I heard a car door open, and looked to my left to see a car parked a short way down the street. The driver, a tall dark-haired man, was running towards us.

'Andie. Thank God you're okay.' The young man wrapped her in his arms when he drew near.

His eyes scanned the rest of us over her head. 'We need to get you guys the hell away from here. It won't take the cops long to figure out where you went.'

He led us back to the car, with Andie taking the front passenger seat, and Angel, Daniel and I crowding into the back. I was in the middle, Daniel's warm body pressed against my side, his arm wrapped around my shoulder. I wanted to sink into him, let the feel of him chase away the fear. But I held myself upright, staring blindly off into the night as I waited for an outcry that signalled we had been discovered.

Angel leaned forward and placed a hand on Andie's arm. 'I know where we can hide.' With her giving directions to Nick via Andie, she led us several streets over, to a new-looking brick house with a bright red letter box.

'The owners are away and there's a key hidden under the flowerpot near the back door. There's a large shed in the back where Nick can hide his car,' said Angel.

Nick navigated down a narrow driveway running alongside the two-storey house, stopping with the engine running as Daniel got out of the car to open the shed door. Angel, Andie and I got out before Nick drove the car into the shed, and I winced at the loud noise the roller door made as it clanged shut. But there was no outcry as we made our way to the back door and Angel found the key hidden under a flowerpot, just where she'd said it would be.

She'd said I was like her, but her ability to know things, and to find us a safe place, was amazing compared with what I could do. I couldn't control the energy that built up inside me, and couldn't direct the lightning when it shot out of my fingertips. All the power had done was make me a target for the doctor who had tortured me, according to the others. But was this a new thing, or had I been able to create lightning before I'd become catatonic?

Was that the medical condition I'd been receiving treatment for?

I only had Angel and Andie's word that the doctor in my waking nightmare was from the estate. What if that doctor had been the one who'd made me like this and the ones at the estate were only trying to help me?

Had I done the right thing by fleeing and coming to Angel?

I was swept into the house along with the others, struggling to make sense of it all. From the moment I had the vision of Angel, and heard her name, I'd been sure she was the answer. But when I'd finally been able to connect with her there'd been no miraculous return of my memories or anything else. Yes, I felt safe with these people, especially Daniel, connected to them in same inexplicable way, but that didn't mean it was right.

Then again, with no memory to guide me, I had to rely on my instinct, and it was telling me these people were good. I had to trust that I was where I was supposed to be, for now at least. It wasn't like I had many other options to choose from in any case.

A flicker of light caught my eye, dragging me from my thoughts, and I looked over to see Andie had found a candle and some matches in one of the kitchen drawers. She lit the candle and placed it on a breakfast bar, shrugging when she caught me watching her. 'I thought it would be a good idea to avoid bright lights. Don't want the neighbours getting suspicious about sudden activity in a supposedly empty house. We should keep the noise to a minimum too.'

Angel's eyes held a faraway expression, head tilted to the

side, as she said, 'We'll be fine here for the night, but we will need to find a new place to hide tomorrow.'

'In that case, let's see what these guys have in the way of hot drinks,' said Andie as she bustled around the kitchen opening cupboards. 'I barely got a sip of my coffee. I need a caffeine jolt if I'm going to be able to stay awake to help figure out what we should do next.'

'What are we going to do next?' Nick asked, grabbing five mugs out of the cupboard above where the kettle was plugged in and setting them down on the bench. 'That crazy doctor isn't the type to give up easily. She won't stop until she has all three of you back at the Wo–'

Andie spun around and placed a finger on his mouth. 'Don't say that name. Or the crazy doctor's name. Gets a bad reaction from Celeste, and we don't want the people who live here to come home and find all their lightbulbs shattered.' She gave me a rueful smile. 'No offence.'

'It's fine,' I said, working to relax the muscles in my neck that had tensed up while Nick was talking. 'I'm going to have to learn to control my response sooner or later. But you're right. It shouldn't be here, in someone else's home. Bad enough we've broken in and are stealing their coffee.'

'Hot chocolate,' said Daniel, as he surveyed the contents of the large corner pantry. 'Doesn't look as though these people drink coffee.' He handed a tin of chocolate powder to Nick and then opened the fridge to get the milk out.

'And technically, we didn't break in,' said Nick. His smile revealed dimples on either side of his mouth. 'Angel found the key. No breaking required.'

'We won't stay here a minute longer than we have to,' said Andie as she made the drinks and handed them out. 'Just long enough to plan our next move, and for the police to clear the area.'

I held my mug of hot chocolate in both hands, relishing

the warmth even though a thread of guilt fizzed in my stomach at stealing from the people whose house we had taken shelter in. But the rich scent of the chocolate was too much to resist. I took a sip, delighting in the sweetness as it slid down my throat, warming me up from the inside out.

I tried to block out the soft murmur of words as Andie explained to Nick everything that had happened since I'd arrived on their doorstep.

When she was finished, Nick asked, 'How come the police only mentioned Celeste being missing, and not you and Angel? Why wouldn't the crazy doctor have put out a missing person's report for you guys too?'

'I guess she took Angel's threat to burn the place down seriously,' said Andie. 'And she knows where we live. I'm guessing she would never have involved the police if she realised Celeste was with us. She'd have just sent her creepy orderlies and the security guards after us again.'

'She will never give up,' said Angel. 'The three of us represent everything she's been working for. She won't stop until she has us in her grasp again.'

I shivered at her words, leaving it for Andie to tell Daniel and Nick what she had said. Daniel gave me a reassuring smile. My smile in response may have trembled slightly, but at least I could form one.

'Okay then, we have two things we need to figure out. Where to go from here and how to make sure the girls are safe, permanently.' Nick looked determined as he glanced over at Andie. 'I am not letting that doctor get her hands on you ever again.' He shifted to look over at Angel. 'Or you.'

'Or Celeste,' said Daniel. 'She's suffered too.'

'We're not the only ones who need protecting,' I said, deciding it was time I spoke up and did something other than just follow along blindly. 'What about all the other kids in that place? We have no idea what she's been doing to them.'

'Celeste is right,' said Angel. 'We aren't the only ones she tortured. She used shock treatment whenever she thought she could get away with it, to study the effect it had on developing brains. We have to stop her hurting any other kids.'

'So, we get her shut down.' Andie placed her mug on the bench. 'Discredit her. It's the only way we can ever have normal lives.'

While I agreed with the sentiment, and that the crazy doctor had to be stopped, the thought of living a normal life was bittersweet.

How could I possibly have a chance at being normal when I didn't even know who I was?

6

'The doctor may be crazy, but she wasn't wrong when she said we can't afford a lawyer,' said Daniel. 'Or about contacting the media. I can just imagine the kind of frenzy it would create if word got out about Angel and Celeste and the things they can do. Any chance of a normal life would be dead and buried, even if we did manage to get the estate shut down and the doctor discredited. We have to figure out a way of stopping her that doesn't require us going public.'

I shuddered at the images his words created in my mind, of Angel and me being hounded by the media, people wanting us to show them our powers, or hating us for having them. Daniel was right. Going public was not an option.

'How are we supposed to achieve that?' Nick scratched at his head. 'Andie said she had her reputation ruined years ago by some kid who faked having psychic powers, and the humiliation was what was driving her to prove her theories were correct. They knocked her down, and she bounced back bigger and crazier than ever. Whatever we do needs to be permanent, giving her no chance to come back and haunt us or hurt any more of her patients.'

'What about the police? Do you think they would help us?' Andie sounded uncertain.

'Not without proof,' I said.

'There is proof, at the estate,' said Angel, indigo gaze haunted by her memories. 'She documented everything she did to me to ensure no one would be able to ridicule her research. She had a camera set up to film each session.' She swallowed heavily, looking over at me before continuing. 'It's in the room where they do the electric shock therapy.'

I choked down bile as memory fragments of the time I'd spent in that room slammed into me, stealing my breath. I couldn't afford to let the nightmare drag me under again; not if I wanted to be free.

I sucked air back into my lungs, hardly able to believe the words about to exit my mouth. 'We have to go back to the estate, and find those tapes. We need concrete evidence to show the police what she does to her patients. Then they will have no choice but to listen to us and see she is shut down for good.'

I put my mug on the bench, so it wouldn't give away how much my hands were shaking at the thought of going back there. I crossed my arms in front of me, struggling to keep my expression neutral.

Daniel moved closer to me as he said, 'Celeste is right. Without proof, the police will just hand her straight back to the crazy doctor.'

He faced me. 'But you don't have to go anywhere near the estate.' He glanced at his sisters. 'That goes for the two of you as well. Nick and I can get the proof we need. You never need to set foot in that place again.'

I lifted my chin, and attempted a smile. 'Yes, I do.'

I may not have any memories of my past life, but I knew I couldn't start to live my new life if I was constantly looking over my shoulder, waiting for the crazy doctor to pounce. There was no way the five of us could remain hidden forever. Sooner or later we would be found. Andie, Angel and I would be dragged back to the estate, and Daniel and Nick would probably wind up in jail for helping us. The only way to prevent that was to face my demons and find enough evidence to set us all free.

I could tell from Angel and Andie's determined faces they also knew this was our only option. Not that it meant they

159

liked it any more than I did! The thought of returning to where I had been tortured was almost enough to send me catatonic again, but I'd do it.

Angel nodded as Andie said, 'There's no way we're staying behind. Angel is the only one who knows where the room is, and neither of you can hear her.'

'She can give us directions, and draw a map,' said Daniel. 'I don't want any of you to go back there. It's too dangerous. You could get caught. If anything happened to you ...' His voice petered out as he looked from his sisters to me, expression stricken. 'I don't want you to be hurt ever again.'

'I'm with Daniel. You three should stay here, where it's safe.' Nick wrapped his arms around Andie. 'Daniel and I can handle this.'

Andie cupped Nick's face in her palms. 'No, you can't. You need us with you. Directions and a map are no substitute for firsthand knowledge. Besides, you saw what Angel and I can do when we're together, and Celeste has some nifty tricks up her sleeve too. We do this together, or we don't do it at all.'

'Andie's right. We all need to do this,' I told Daniel, 'and maybe I'll be able to find out more about who I am while we're there. There must be paperwork with the details of my admission on it. It would have next of kin information. I'll be able to track down my family, and find out why I was at the estate.'

Of course, if my family were the ones who'd sent me there in the first place then maybe I'd be better off not finding them.

No. I had to find out who I was. It was the only way to move forward.

The concern didn't leave Daniel's eyes, but he gave a nod. 'So that's it,' he said. 'We break into the estate and find the tapes to prove the crazy doctor has been torturing the patients in her care. Then we go to the police and get her arrested.'

'When do we want to do this?' Andie asked.

'Now,' I said, knowing I needed to do this before I lost my courage.

Angel seconded me, a determined look in her eyes.

Daniel ran a hand through his hair, mussing it up. 'It could work. They wouldn't be expecting us to return, not so soon after you girls all escaped. We'd have the element of surprise at least.'

'I shorted out the power, as I was escaping,' I said with a rueful shrug. 'With luck, they haven't got it fixed yet.'

'Okay then, let's see if we can find torches,' said Andie. 'We don't want to be stumbling around in the dark.'

We searched the house, found a collection of torches of varying sizes and raided the home owners' wardrobes to outfit us more appropriately for a stealth mission. Guilt again fizzed in my stomach at the thought of taking stuff that didn't belong to me, but I forced it down with the promise to return everything I took. I slipped a fitted black jacket on over the Wonder Woman shirt Andie had loaned me. I even found a pair of shoes to borrow. They were loose, but better than going barefoot.

Luckily, my hair was now dry. I combed it through with my fingers and braided it as tightly as I could. I secured the end with a rubber band from a bunch of catalogues I found on the kitchen counter, smiling as Angel and Andie did the same.

Once we were prepared, we piled back into Nick's car and headed off down the street. We all kept a wary eye out for police cars as he drove us to a friend's house on the other side of town. Once we arrived, he let us out on the footpath before parking his car in the backyard. Then he went inside to borrow the keys for his friend's 4WD.

We had no way of knowing if the police knew Nick was

161

involved in my disappearance. But the crazy doctor and the men who worked for her had seen his car when he and Daniel rescued Angel and Andie that morning. A 4WD was also going to come in handy once we reached our destination, as a sedan wasn't built for off-road driving.

As we drew near the estate, travelling along the road I had run down earlier that day, the tension returned tenfold. It was hard to sit still and accept I was willingly going back there. Angel and Andie sat either side of me and in unison they reached out and grabbed my hands. I fought not to cry, immensely grateful for their support. I had no doubt they were just as anxious as me about what was going to happen next.

Holding hands, we sat in silence as Nick turned the 4WD off the road and began cutting his way through the bush running alongside the high mesh fence bordering the estate. He worked his way along it until we were near the back corner.

He applied the brakes and cut the engine. 'We walk from here,' he said.

I let go of Angel's and Andie's hands as we climbed out of the vehicle. We stood side by side and looked towards the estate. We were still some distance away from the main building, with dozens of trees blocking the view, but I saw a glimmer of lights in some of the windows.

'The power is back on,' I said, shoulders slumping. Obviously, whatever it was I did to short it out had not been as difficult to fix as I'd hoped.

'The fence will be electrified,' said Angel. 'We won't be able to get inside until that's taken care of.'

As Andie told Daniel and Nick about the electric fence, Angel turned to me. 'Do you think you'll be able to short out the fence?'

I shrugged. 'I have no idea how to control whatever it is I can do, but I'll try.'

162

Torches pointed to the ground to minimise the threat of detection, we wound our way through the bush to the fence. I handed my torch to Daniel, managing a smile for him when he gave my hand a squeeze, and asked them all to get behind me.

I faced the fence, sucking in several deep breaths as I stretched out my hands, fingers pointing at the fence. I bit my bottom lip as I struggled to remember what it felt like when sparks shot out of my fingers into the keypad.

Then, I'd been panicked, desperate, every ounce of my being focused on escape. The frustration of being unable to break free causing a build-up of energy inside me. Now, I was still panicked, desperate and frustrated, but the intensity was not the same. I closed my eyes to aid my concentration, focusing as hard as I could on blasting the fence with a lightning bolt.

Nothing happened. I opened my eyes and faced the others. 'I'm sorry. It's not working. I have no idea what I'm doing.'

'Let us help you,' said Angel as she moved to stand beside me. She took my left hand as Andie moved up to take the right. We faced the electric fence together, Angel keeping up a constant murmur of words in my head, telling me to focus everything I had on a section of the fence directly in front of us.

At first nothing changed, we were just three girls linked by our hands, standing in front of a fence. But then, the hands clasping mine began to feel warmer, more so than could be explained by combined body heat. The warm sensation spread up my arms, wrapping around my torso and quickly spreading to every inch of my body. Once every part of me felt as if I'd been immersed in a hot air vent, the sensation changed, becoming more of a tingle.

I felt static electricity in the air seconds before sparks

appeared in front of me. The hands holding mine tightened their grip when the blue-white sparks grew more numerous, but their connection with me seemed to protect my companions from harm.

For me, the sparks were a welcome sight, a sign I could in fact do this. I didn't need Angel's prompting to draw them to me, collecting them in the air in front of me until they became one sparking, shining ball of energy.

It pulsed in time with my heartbeat, coalescing into a tight sphere packed with energy. I knew the instant it was stable enough to use, acting on instinct, using the power of my mind to fling the sphere at the spot in the fence I had been staring at earlier. It hit the mesh, blue-white sparks flying every which way. The current flowed along the fence panel. It travelled for some distance on either side of the section I had targeted before it finally died. I could no longer feel the call of it in my blood, though my body still hummed with extra energy.

'Did it work?'

I let go of Angel and Andie's hands and looked over my shoulder at Daniel. 'Only one way to find out,' I said as I stretched my hand out to touch the fence.

7

The mesh fence was warm to the touch, but no electric current flowed through it.

'It worked,' I said, facing the others with a satisfied smile.

'You know, there are safer ways to check if it was still electrified than touching the damn thing,' said Daniel, shaking his head.

I ignored his grumpy tone, realising worry for me had him sounding so out of sorts. Despite the fact we were attempting to break into a place I had only recently escaped from, where I had been subjected to electric shock therapy, I felt good. Alive. It was hard to keep the smile from my face as I watched the guys get to work cutting a hole in the fence with tools they'd found in the shed where we'd first hidden Nick's car.

Once they'd cut a hole large enough for us to slip through one at a time, and the extra energy filling my body dissipated, some of my enthusiasm flagged. Dread pooled in the pit of my stomach, sitting heavily like a stone at the thought of being caught. I forced down my misgivings about what we were attempting to do as we wound our way through the large trees lining the other side of the fence.

Andie looked around her with a dazed expression, torchlight dancing around the tree trunks. 'This is the place from my vision,' she said, reaching out to take Angel's hand. 'This is where I saw you, when you first called out for me to help you.'

Angel nodded, and I could see the shine of tears in her eyes. 'Yes. This is where I finally found you, after so many years of trying.'

Tears shimmered in Andie's eyes as well, as she hugged her twin. 'I'm sorry it took me so long to remember you.'

I felt like crying too, at the thought of what Angel and Andie had endured. Was there someone out there who missed me as much as they had missed one another? Andie had been drugged for fifteen years to get her to forget her twin sister existed, yet her dreams had done their best to remind her. I had no way of knowing if one day I too would be reunited with someone who loved me as much as Daniel and Andie loved Angel.

Breaking into the estate, finding the paperwork from my admission, was the first step in finding my family. Andie said her memories returned after she'd touched Angel for the first time. I hoped that once I got the chance to meet my family, to reach out and touch them, I would remember who I was. But none of that would happen if we didn't get moving.

Before I could say anything, Nick moved over to Andie and Angel and tapped them both on the arm. 'As wonderful as this trip down memory lane is, it's not what we came for. Time to get moving. The longer we hang around out here, the more chance there is of someone looking out a window and spotting us or the light from our torches. Time to go dark.'

We switched off our torches, relying on the light of the full moon to guide us as we crept to the edge of the trees. The estate loomed over us; a large, squat building made of a dark grey stone, three storeys high, all the windows barred. In between us and the building was an expanse of manicured lawn. On the other side of the lawn, closer to the building, was a sprawling garden with winding paths and flower beds. Gazebos were scattered throughout the garden, with seats for the patients to relax and admire the view. It was probably a tranquil space in the light of day, but at night it was a shadow-filled minefield for us to cross.

Daniel came over to stand beside me and we set out across the lawn, crouching low, making for the closest gazebo. The others were close on our heels and as we ran, the only sound was our breathing and the soft tread of our footsteps in the grass. Once we reached the gazebo we stopped to orientate ourselves, searching the windows for any sign of activity and to ensure we hadn't been seen before we moved on to the next one.

Eventually we reached the gazebo closest to the building, and my eyes followed the path from the gazebo entrance to the back door.

Daniel leaned in close, his breath raising a shiver as it caressed the skin of my neck. 'Are you ready for this?'

No.

'Yes,' I said, grateful for the shadows camouflaging my blush at his proximity.

He gave my shoulder a squeeze as the others crowded around us, ready for the dash to the back door.

The door opened, and a male orderly in a blue uniform stepped outside.

We ducked as one, retreating to the shadows coating the gazebo as we watched the orderly light up a cigarette. It seemed to take forever for him to finish it, and my gaze was caught by the orange tip of his cigarette when it flared brighter each time he lifted it to his lips and inhaled. Finally, he dropped the butt on the ground and stubbed it out with his boot before kicking it into the flowerbed on his left.

I thought he would go back inside then, but he remained where he was, hands shoved into his pockets, staring out into the darkened garden. Excruciating minutes passed with me not daring to move, conscious of Daniel's arm wrapped around my waist where we huddled in the corner of the gazebo. I focused on the orderly, determined not to think about how nice it felt to be in Daniel's arms. I wanted to move closer, snuggle in, and have him wrap his other arm around me.

I forced myself to remain still. I couldn't afford to get attached to Daniel. What if I got my memory back and discovered I had a boyfriend waiting for me. Better to not let myself get carried away by the situation, and the level of care Daniel showed toward me, than to risk hurting him down the track.

Slowly, so it wouldn't alert the orderly to our presence, I moved as far away from Daniel as I could in the limited space. Time to stand on my own two feet and take responsibility for myself.

Daniel turned to look at me when I eased myself out from under his arm, a query he couldn't safely voice in his eyes. I gave him a smile, hoping it appeared confident and calm. Inside, I felt bereft at losing contact with him. I lifted my chin and indicated toward the door, where a second orderly had joined the first.

This guy was huge, brutish, with long blond hair caught in a low ponytail. I felt Andie stiffen on the other side of me, a low hiss emerging from her lips. Clearly, she was not fond of this guy. I didn't blame her. Even with so little light to see by, something in his demeanour shouted bully.

'Hey,' he said, voice low and menacing, carrying easily in the still night air. 'We don't pay you to stand around basking in the moonlight. Get your arse back inside and make sure all the little retards are locked in their rooms. Don't want any of them wandering around in the middle of the night.'

The smaller orderly ducked his head, not making eye contact, shoulders hunched as he headed back inside. The large orderly remained where he was for a moment, looking over the garden. His gaze passed over the gazebo and I forgot to breathe as I waited for him to spot us. But he obviously found nothing amiss and soon headed inside.

I stood, legs shaking, dizzy from holding my breath for so long, and made myself walk to the opening of the gazebo. I didn't wait for the others to join me, but sprinted to the back door. Once there, I tested the handle, pleased to find it unlocked. With my nerves all in a tangle, I didn't think I had it in me to attempt to use whatever power I possessed to break in.

The others crowded at my back as I turned the handle and slowly pushed the door open.

It opened onto a short hallway with closed doors on either side. According to Angel, these were storage rooms. The rest of the ground floor was taken up by the common room I'd woken up in and the front foyer area. Between the two main areas was a kitchen and dining area where patients who were mobile ate their meals, as well as a lunchroom for the staff. The first floor was where the medical personnel had offices and treatment rooms, while the patients were housed on the second floor.

The real action took place below ground. The first of the lower levels contained the crazy doctor's hidden office. The level below was where the treatment rooms for her special cases were, where the shock treatment was administered. Angel had spent long periods of time locked up on the third level below ground, in a soundproof room. It had become her permanent home ever since she had escaped six months ago.

Before then she had been allowed to sit in on lessons for the other patients who had been there long term, and share a room with one of the girls. As a reward for good behaviour she'd even been allowed to walk in the gardens at night, at least until she'd used that time to try to escape and contact Andie.

The times she had been allowed to mingle with the other patients, she had never met me. Therefore, I must have been brought here after she'd been punished with no further trips above ground during the day. If that was the case, I had spent less than six months in the crazy doctor's hands, while she had been trapped in this place for fifteen long and lonely years.

Poor Angel. It must have taken so much courage for her to return here, after everything she endured. My fear was nothing compared with hers.

I straightened my shoulders, ready to get this done.

We'd planned this out beforehand, so there was no need to discuss what we were to do next. Considering the nature of her research, and the fact she was torturing some of her patients, we figure the doctor wouldn't leave incriminating files or tapes in her main office on the second floor. What we were searching for must be below ground.

Angel took the lead, stopping every so often to test the area ahead of us, making sure the way was clear. With her help, we reached the elevators just outside the common room. We slipped past them, heading for the set of stairs Andie and Angel had used to escape earlier that day. They stood side by side, holding hands, as Angel placed her free hand on the keypad.

I sensed the energy flowing through and around them, seeing a quiver in the air as they both focused on the lock. A shiver swept over my body at the quiet snick as the display went from red to green.

Angel turned the handle and pushed the door open, showing no hesitation as she stepped into the darkened stairwell, still holding Andie's hand. I swallowed my nerves and followed, with Daniel and Nick at my heels. The door closed behind us, shutting out the light from the common room.

My breathing sped up, eyes struggling to adjust to the darkness. Only a dim emergency light lit the stairwell. Even when we switched on our torches, it still felt as if the darkness was hemming me in, suffocating me. The slow pace we set as we trooped down the stairs to the next level was torturous.

I wanted to run, bound down the stairs two or three at a time, and get out of there as fast as I possibly could, but was painfully aware to do so might alert the staff working the nightshift. My breathing came faster and faster, the sound of it magnified by the enclosed space of the stairwell. Sparks arced from my fingertips and I whimpered, sure I was about to set off an explosion of lightning that would doom us all.

A firm hand settled on my shoulder, stopping my forward momentum. Daniel turned me around to face him. With me on the step above him, we were at eye level. He passed his torch to Nick and then brought his hands up to my face, gently stroking my cheeks as he gazed into my eyes.

'Take deep breaths,' he said, voice barely above a whisper. 'Focus on me, and just breathe.'

I sagged against him. This time I didn't worry about taking advantage of his kindness. I needed this. Needed him, if I was going to get through whatever happened next. Slowly and steadily, as I concentrated on my breathing, the tight band around my chest eased and the energy surging through me dissipated. But I was still conscious of it, close to the surface, and hoped nothing else happened to upset the equilibrium

The sooner we found what we were looking for, and got out of here, the better.

8

I eased away from Daniel, took a deep breath and gave a nod to Andie and Angel who were poised a couple of steps below me, to indicate I was ready to move on. I kept my eyes focused on the backs of their heads as we made our way down the stairs to a small landing for the exit to the first level below ground. This was where the doctor had her main office, and where I hoped I'd find out who I really was.

No keypad barred access on this side of the door, and there was nothing to prevent Andie from just opening it and stepping out into the small alcove containing the emergency exit and the elevator. Daniel held the door open for me and then crouched to place his torch in the gap to stop it from locking behind us.

Hands slick with sweat, I wiped my torch on my shirt and slipped it into my back pocket, sure it would slip out of my hands otherwise. The level was in darkness, the light of the other three torches and the emergency lighting more than sufficient to illuminate our way as the five of us filed out of the stairwell and gathered at the start of a short hall.

Unlike the sprawling main building above ground, the lower level was small, with only two doors on the left side of the hall and one on the right. All three doors were closed, and Nick shone his torch over the sign on the first door on the left. It was the unisex sign for a bathroom. From this far away, it wasn't possible to read the sign on the second door on the left, but it didn't matter.

The door we wanted was to the right of us.

A sign was at eye level, embossed with the name Dr

Joanna Wood.

A chill swept over me at the sight of the doctor's name, and I was hard pressed to keep hold of my newfound equilibrium. I wanted to scream, to shout out a warning as Angel stretched out her hand and turned the door handle. Instead I clamped my jaw tight, determined not to cry out as the door opened easily at her touch.

Angel slipped inside the room, with Andie close behind her, but I couldn't move. I couldn't force my legs to take the steps that would carry me across the threshold.

'You don't have to do this,' said Daniel, the sound of his voice soothing some of the tension inside my body as Nick brushed past us to join Andie and Angel.

I gulped down my fear, lifting my chin and managing to give him a tight smile. 'Yes, I do. The faster we get this place searched, and find what we came for, the sooner we can get the hell out of here.'

I would not let fear paralyse me. I dug my nails into my palms and forced first one leg and then the other to move, not stopping until I was in the middle of the room.

Daniel closed the door behind us, and then switched on a light.

The office was one large open space, sparsely furnished with a utilitarian desk at one end, and row after row of bookcases down the other. Behind the desk was an interactive whiteboard, the screen blank, the computer to power it nowhere to be seen. Along the wall opposite the doorway stood filing cabinets of varying sizes and colours, and it was to these the others had been drawn. I hurried over to join them, forcing my fingers to relax as I tried to open the top drawer of the filing cabinet closest to the desk.

Unlike the door to the office, the filing cabinets were locked. Nick and Daniel produced screwdrivers from their back pockets, and set to work jimmying each filing cabinet open. After Daniel broke into the cabinet I had selected, and moved on to the next one, I started my search for answers.

I frowned as I read the file names on the tabs for each folder in the top drawer. None of it made sense. Was it code, or medical jargon? I pulled one of the folders free, moving over to the desk so I could spread the contents out to see if I could make any sense of them.

All I found were lists of medications, with suggested dosages as well as the expected effects and side effects. A search through the rest of the drawers in the cabinet revealed much of the same, years' worth of medical documents relating to the treatment of adolescents with behavioural issues. This was exactly what one would expect to find in a place supposedly dedicated to the treatment of children and teenagers.

The next cabinet held research material, my frustration growing each time I opened a new folder and came up empty. I sighed, looking around to see discouraged expressions on the faces of the others once we had searched every single cabinet, and done a quick check of the bookshelves as well.

'She must keep the files on the next floor down, where the treatment rooms are,' said Angel. Trepidation laced the words in my head, and her expression was grim.

She wasn't looking forward to returning to the place where the doctor had carried out secret tests any more than I was. Yet, she was still determined to carry through on the plan, despite having spent far longer here than I had. If she could be that brave, then so could I. I headed out the door, and waited for the others to join me in the hallway.

Daniel exited last of all, switching off the light in the office before closing the door. He walked over to the exit door leading to the stairwell, stopping once he realised I wasn't following him. I had remained where I was, staring at the sign on the office door.

Dr Joanna Wood.

I read the name repeatedly, steeling myself not to react. My skin tingled as the energy in my body surged, but I refused to let it take over, stamping down on it as I focused on the name and the nightmarish mental image it provoked.

Dr Joanna Wood, long brown hair pulled back in a tight ponytail, lab coat over her clothes, a detached expression on her face as she hit the button that sent agonising jolts of electricity through my body again and again.

Fists clenched at my sides, muscles tense, I turned my back on the sign and walked over to where Daniel waited for me with a quizzical look.

'I won't let her control me anymore. She has taken enough from me,' I said, chin raised.

He didn't speak, simply nodded and took my hand as we slipped through the exit door and took the stairs to the level below.

Angel, Andie and Nick were waiting on the landing for us. Nick opened the door and once again Daniel used his torch to prop it open after we had all passed through. We stepped to the start of the small hallway, to find it was set out exactly the same as the level above. Once again, it was the single door to the right that held our attention.

This door had a keypad barring entry, and a glass panel set at eye height.

I saw Angel's hand shaking as she reached out to touch the keypad, and Andie was quick to take her other hand. Acting on instinct, I moved to stand behind them, placing my hands on Angel's shoulders. My hands tingled, warmth flowing through my body, and I gasped as a connection opened between the three of us.

I could feel them, feel the deep reservoir of power Andie held as she opened a channel to allow Angel to access it. Angel drew on the power, her control fine and careful as she sent it into the keypad and disengaged the lock. Andie tugged on the door handle, twisting it open, and I reluctantly let my hands fall from Angel's shoulders. For that short time I'd felt connected, part of something, no longer a stranger to myself.

I sucked in a deep breath as an intense longing to be part of something similar hit. Would I ever get the chance to experience that level of trust and connection, to know without hesitation or fear the other person was there for me the way Andie and Angel were there for one another?

Daniel stepped up beside me, holding the door open as he waited for me to step through. I gave him a tremulous smile, suddenly on the verge of tears. I refused to let them fall, ducking my head so he wouldn't see the tell-tale sheen in my eyes as I walked past him. I stumbled into the room, eyes unfocused. I bumped into something in my path and put out my hands to clutch at a cold metal bar, wrapping my fingers around it to ground myself. I dropped my gaze, focusing on what I held on to, and gasped.

A hospital-issue bed, mattress covered in a white sheet, sat in front of me. A lump settled in my throat at the sight of straps used for holding a patient in place. My vision glazed over, a nightmare hovering on the fringe of my awareness, but I pushed it back to look around the rest of the room.

There was a second bed beside the one I had banged into. The other one also had the straps attached to the metal sides, the nearest of which had been lowered to allow the doctor and her staff to load a patient onto the bed. Bright rectangular lights were positioned directly above each bed, and a console sat on wheeled tables to the right. My eyes fixed on the wires coming out of the nearest console, on the dials and buttons to adjust the voltage of electricity used to treat the patient.

No. Not patient. Victim.

What happened in this room was not medicine.

I looked over to Angel. She appeared to be similarly

transfixed by the sight of the beds and the apparatus used to torture us. As if she felt my gaze she looked over at me, expression solemn but determined. As one we turned away from the beds, denying them any hold over us, and looked over the rest of the room.

The room was split into two sections. The front section contained the beds, with a desk positioned nearby so the doctor would be able to observe her victims at close hand. The back section of the room was screened off by a thick black curtain. Nick slipped behind the curtain and then called out for Andie to join him. Angel followed her twin, while I headed for the desk.

The top of the desk was bare, and I hoped that was because anything of interest was kept inside the drawers. There were two smaller drawers set on top of a larger one suitable for storing files. I reached out to open the bottom one.

Locked.

'Here, let me try,' said Daniel, gently ushering me to the side as he set to work jimmying the lock. Within moments he had the drawer open, then stepped back so I could be the first to look inside.

Unlike the filing cabinets in the room above, which had been stuffed with papers, this drawer held just three folders. I grabbed them out of the drawer and laid them flat on the desk, staring at the label emblazed on all three; "Arcane Abilities Research Program". The names printed out in neat writing on the tab attached to the top of each file sent chills racing over my body.

Subject A - Angela Sherman.

Subject B - Andrea Sherman.

Subject C - Celeste Wood.

I heard Daniel calling my name, but it sounded faint, barely recognisable, as if he was calling out to me from an immeasurable distance.

Celeste Wood.

Dr Joanna Wood.

The Wood Estate.

God, no. It had to be a mistake.

I handed the folder to Daniel, so he could read what the tab said, my eyes imploring him to tell me it didn't say what I thought it did. I needed him to tell me it was a coincidence my last name and the name of the crazy doctor who had tortured his sisters and me was the same. His expression was stricken as he looked from the name to me.

He opened his mouth to say something, but never got the chance. Another voice chimed in first, the sound of it setting a shudder over my entire body.

9

'Welcome home, Celeste.'

I turned to face the door, the shudders racking my body intensifying as I looked at Dr Joanna Wood. She stood just inside the doorway, flanked by the brutish orderly and a second one who was almost as big as him. They were blocking the exit, making escape impossible.

Dr Wood's smile was cool. 'What, aren't you even going to say hello to your mother?'

I shook my head, finally finding my voice. 'You're not my mother.'

'Really, Celeste, after everything I've done for you, you're going to disown me?' She gave a laugh that held not even a hint of humour. 'It doesn't work that way, sweetheart. I am your mother, whether you like it or not. Nothing will ever change that.'

'Everything you've done for me?' My words were a screech. 'You strapped me down and tortured me. You electrocuted me, and just stood there taking notes. What kind of mother tortures her own child?'

'Stop being so melodramatic. What I did was for your own good. And electroconvulsive therapy is hardly torture. It is an established treatment for those with severe depression who cannot be helped with more traditional methods.' She stepped farther into the room, indicating for the orderlies to stay by the door.

'You were sick. Suicidal. You needed help, and I took care of you.'

I shook my head, backing away from her words. 'That

can't be. I am not depressed or suicidal. You're lying.'

Her eyebrows arched. 'Why would I lie about something like that?'

'To confuse me. To try and make me think you're not the bad guy. To stop me going to the authorities and having you shut down. I was catatonic, because of what you did to me.' I clenched my hands, pushing them into my sides, nails digging into my palms so the sparks shooting out of my fingertips would not be visible. My body twitched, aching to release the energy roaring through me from the first sound of her voice.

'I did what you asked me to do. Don't you remember? You were miserable, unable to function. You begged me to help you. So of course, I did everything in my power to make you better.' She took another step closer. 'And the treatment was working. You were improving to the point I believed we would be able to control your depression with medication. But two months ago you insisted on one more round of ECT, to make sure.'

She shook her head, plastering a sad expression on her face, inching forward once more. 'I should never have given in, but you were so determined. I had no way of knowing the last session we did would cause you to shut down.'

I had backed up as far as I could, banging into one of the beds, Daniel keeping pace with me. He kept shooting worried glances my way, but appeared content to let me handle this.

I urged caution in response to a silent query from Angel, hidden behind the curtain with Andie and Nick. Now was not the time to act. The orderlies still blocked the doorway, forming a formidable barrier we would have to force our way through to have any hope of escape. I had to draw them away, get them to join Dr Wood in the middle of the room.

I couldn't think of her as my mother, still not convinced it wasn't a vicious lie created to torment me further.

'Celeste,' she said, hands raised in a plea, 'you must

believe me. I only did what you wanted me to do. I never wanted to hurt you.'

'I would never ask you to do that to me. Never. No sane person would ever willingly subject themselves to being electrocuted.'

'Sweetheart, you were mentally ill, and we had already tried every other method of treatment available. When it became a choice of ECT, or being locked away in an institution for the rest of your life to prevent you from hurting either yourself or others, you chose this. Surely you remember the counselling sessions we underwent before we came to this decision?'

'No. That's not true. It can't be.'

She sounded reasonable, so sure of herself, and if I didn't know better I might have fallen for her lies. As it was, each lie that fell from her lips only served to agitate the energy building up inside of me until I felt I would explode with it. Only the thought that I had to make sure the others were safe allowed me to maintain a smidge of control.

'You really don't remember, do you?' A small smile played around her lips, but she quickly regained her pose of motherly concern. 'Of course, now it all makes sense. One of the possible side effects of ECT is retrograde amnesia, where you lose the memory of recent events. We discussed this at length before we started the treatment, but you thought it was a small price to pay to make you well again, especially as in most cases the memory improves within a couple of months after treatment ends.'

'No. No. You're lying.' I wrapped my arms around my torso, trying to block out her words, relishing the feel of the sparks shooting into my body, the momentary warmth they gave off helping to negate the chill her words engendered. 'Electrocuting someone over and over again until they go catatonic and lose their memory is not therapy. It's torture.'

A cool smile curved her lips. 'From what I understand, the therapy you are so upset about is what elevated you from an ordinary girl to one with potential psychic abilities. You should be thanking me for lifting you out of obscurity.'

Disgust filled my mouth with bile. I grimaced as I swallowed it down.

'Listen to you. You're a monster. You were experimenting on me, as you did on Angel and Andie. You were trying to turn us into a freak show so you can be famous and restore your shitty reputation. It was never about helping me.'

Anger flared in her eyes, her next attempt at appearing to care reeking of insincerity. 'Oh, Celeste, is that what he's been telling you?' She waved a hand in Daniel's direction. 'He's using you to get to me. He knows his sisters are unstable, that they are better off here, with me, but he doesn't want to believe it. He thinks he can take care of them himself. But he's wrong, very wrong. They're dangerous. That's why his parents signed their care over to me in the first place.

'I was only studying them, and the things they can do, in an effort to understand how to help them. All I've ever wanted to do is help people. You'd know that, if you didn't have amnesia. When your memories return, you'll see I'm telling the truth. I was always doing what was best for you, and for all the patients in my care.'

It sounded good, in theory, but the longer I stared at her, the more I was sure she was lying. I might not have any memories, but every instinct in my body was screaming at me to run, to get as far away from her as possible. But the two huge orderlies had not budged from the doorway.

Time to make them move.

I reached out to Angel with my mind. 'Get ready,' I said, relying on her to warn Andie and Nick something was about to happen.

I tensed, looking sideways to Daniel to see if he was

prepared for action. He gave a nod, the folder containing my file still gripped in his hand. I looked past him, to a gap in the curtains where the others were peeking through. Dr Wood had not appeared to realise we weren't alone. I hoped her ignorance gave us an edge. If Angel and Andie were ready to use their abilities to help us fight our way free, maybe we stood a chance after all.

The success of my hastily formed escape plan hinged on getting the orderlies away from the door.

I looked towards them, at the fluorescent lighting directly above their heads.

I nudged Daniel with my shoulder, to signal my readiness to make a move.

Dr Wood must have sensed her platitudes were falling on deaf ears, and her expression was now one of barely concealed anger. 'Enough of this nonsense, Celeste. I am your mother and I can do whatever I want to you.'

She cast a disparaging look at Daniel. 'And don't think he can save you. He can't even save his own sisters. I'll soon have them back here, locked up in rooms right across the hall from yours. Once I'm done, the three of you will regret ever crossing me, and your new boyfriend will be sitting in jail with his friend, wishing he'd never laid eyes on you.'

I didn't waste time on words. Her threat to put Daniel in jail triggered a surge of energy inside me. I lunged forward, pointing both hands at the fluorescent light closest to the doorway. Ten distinct streams of lightning shot out of my fingertips, arching across the room. One hit the light I'd been aiming at, and the others slammed into the wall and ceiling, setting off a shower of blue-white sparks.

The light instantly blew, glass shards flying every which way. The rest of the lights in the room flickered several times before dying, plunging us into darkness.

The orderlies dived clear of the light exploding above their heads, pushing Dr Wood ahead of them as they moved to get out of the shower of glass. Emergency lighting came on, bathing the room in a pale red glow as I grabbed Daniel by the hand and pulled him toward the now clear doorway. The curtain swished back as the others left their place of concealment and sprinted for the doorway.

'No. Stop them!'

I increased my speed at Dr Wood's shout, not daring to look behind me to see if the orderlies were obeying her or not. I heard a whoosh, then a rush of warmth and light as fire appeared in my peripheral vision. I ground to a halt, looking over to see Dr Wood and the orderlies now trapped behind a wall of fire. Angel held her hand out, controlling the flames, a look of extreme concentration and effort on her face. Andie held her free hand, and I could sense the power flowing out of her and into her twin.

My mouth fell open at the sight. They made my ability to manipulate lightning look like child's play. Daniel tugged on my hand, reminding me I had more important things to worry about. The strain on Andie's face as she fed power to her sister suggested she wouldn't be able to keep it up much longer. We had to get out of there before the fire wall came down.

Nick obviously had the same thought as he grabbed Andie around the waist, reaching out to take Angel's arm at the same time, and backpedalled toward the door.

The fire wall flickered for a long moment before it fell, but by then Daniel and I were outside in the hall, with the others right on our heels. Nick was the last one out, pulling the door shut behind him. I darted forward and placed a hand on the keypad, using a spark of lightning to fry the internal workings.

'That should hold them for a while,' I said, even as loud thumps came from the other side of the door.

'Let's get out of there before they call for help,' said Daniel, the emergency lighting casting ghastly red shadows over his features as he ushered us toward the stairs.

His torch was still propping the door to the stairwell open and we crowded inside. I heard muffled bangs as Dr Wood and the orderlies attempted to break out of the treatment room. Grim satisfaction filled me at the realisation I was the one who had locked them in the room where she had tortured me.

I headed for the stairs to ascend to the ground floor, but stopped when Angel called out for us to wait.

She had her head cocked to the side, staring down the stairs leading to the lowest level, the one where she had been imprisoned for the last six months.

'Something's wrong,' she said in my head, taking a tentative step closer to the lower set of stairs. 'There's something down there.' She looked back at us, weariness etched on her face, shoulders slumped.

Even her voice in my head sounded tired. Producing the wall of fire must have drained her energy. Andie moved to Angel's side, looking as exhausted as her twin as she surveyed the stairs leading to the lowest level.

'Can you sense what it is?' Andie's voice was low, words slow.

'No, I'm too tired to focus.' Angel shook her head. 'I just have this feeling I need to go down there. I don't know why.' She gave a long sigh, straightening her shoulders with visible effort. 'It's gone now, whatever it was.'

'We should keep moving then,' said Nick. 'Before Celeste's mum calls in the reinforcements.'

I winced at his casual use of the term "mum". There was nothing motherly about Dr Joanna Wood. While it may be true she had given birth to me, it took a lot more than that to make her my mother. For once I was glad to have amnesia, sure my history with her was one I would be better off not remembering.

We headed for the stairs to go up. Angel kept glancing back to the stairs to go down, no doubt worrying about whatever it was she had sensed, but she didn't falter as we climbed to ground level. There was no time for talk as we stretched our muscles, my thighs burning with each step. My lungs were also screaming at me to stop but I forced myself to keep going, as I had on my mad dash to get to Angel in the first place. To stop, even for a moment, would make it harder to get going again.

Determined to not lose momentum, I didn't hesitate when we reached ground level, barely pausing as I pushed open the door and ran into the common room. The power was out here as well, but the emergency lighting was enough to see by as we sprinted down the corridor to the back door. Voices called out as we ran, but none of us stopped. Within seconds we reached the back door and burst out into the night.

We made no attempt to hide as we ran across the garden, making for the tree line. Daniel and Nick switched on their torches once we hit the trees, our pace slowing only slightly as we wound our way back to the hole they had made in the fence. We ducked through one at a time, my braid snagging on a piece of wire when it was my turn. Daniel helped me to unwind it, then took my hand as we ran side by side to the 4WD.

Seconds later we piled into the car, buckling our seat belts as Nick got the engine running. Shouts sounded in the distance. I glanced over at the estate to see the two large orderlies, powerful torches in their hands, running towards us with security guards several paces behind them. They were too far away to stop us. I sagged in my seat, slumping against Daniel's shoulder as the enormity of what had just happened hit.

We'd failed.

We had no evidence to take to the police, nothing we could use against my mother. She would be even more determined than ever to get us back, and I had no doubt her threat to see Daniel and Nick put in jail was not an idle one.

We had nowhere to go; no one to help us.

Sooner or later the police would find us, and then Angel, Andie and I would be even worse off than where we started.

10

Nick drove us back to town, pulling into the carpark of the first fast food place on the highway leading into Easton. He didn't cut the engine as he looked to where Angel sat next to me in the back seat.

'Where to from here?'

Angel was slumped against the door, a quiet sigh escaping her lips as she turned her head to face him. 'I don't know. I can't "see" anything at the moment.'

Andie, looking and sounding just as exhausted as her sister, relayed her words to Nick, and then added, 'We have to assume they got the license plate for this car. We can't risk going back to your friend's house.'

'So, we go back to the other house then.'

I felt Daniel shift beside me. 'Angel said we would be safe there until morning. Then we'd have to find somewhere else to hide, and half the night is already gone.'

'I know, but what other option do we have? The girls are in no shape to run around town finding us a new place to hide, even if Angel was able to use her powers to spot an empty house. I say we go back there, crash for a few hours, and then reassess our options.'

'Guess we have no choice,' said Daniel, and I heard his dislike of the idea in his voice.

I didn't blame him. Without Angel's ability to sense what was going to happen, we were travelling blind. But I was so tired, the thought of being caught by the homeowners couldn't compete with my need to sleep. I let my eyes close, resting my head on Daniel's shoulder as Nick drove us out of the carpark. Minutes later, Daniel softly jostled me awake and helped me out of the car.

I allowed him to lead me inside the house, dimly aware of Nick doing the same for Andie. I stumbled over my feet, and would have fallen if not for Daniel's firm arm around my waist. I could barely keep my eyes open as he found one of the bedrooms and helped me onto the bed.

'I'll be back in a minute,' he said as he pulled a blanket over me. 'I need to help Angel.'

I managed a nod, eyes closing of their own accord, and let sleep take me.

Hours later, sun shining through the bedroom window woke me. I struggled to open my eyes and orientate myself, blinking in confusion. The first thing that met my eyes was Daniel, sleeping in an awkward upright position in a chair in the corner of the room. Had he spent the entire night there, watching over me?

A rush of warmth swept over me, accompanied by a flush in my cheeks. After what we'd discovered last night, who I was and how I'd come to be at the estate, I figured there was no boyfriend waiting for me to come home. No one to be hurt if I were to come to care for someone else. Someone like Daniel.

He'd supported me from the start, showing he cared in dozens of little ways, and now I was free to see if his caring had the potential to lead to something more. Not that I planned on jumping into a relationship straight away. But it was nice to wonder what might develop between us once we had dug ourselves out of our current mess.

I sat up and looked around the room, and my stomach fell when I spotted Angel curled up on her side in a single bed, a match to the one I had slept on. Daniel had been watching over both of us.

I pushed down my disappointment at not being the sole object of his protectiveness. Of course, he would be concerned with making sure his sister was okay. He'd thought she was dead for fifteen years, and had only just got her back a day before. It was only natural he would want to watch over her. I was just lucky he had included me by putting us in the same room, when there were three other bedrooms to choose from.

No noises came from the rest of the house, so Nick and Andie must still be asleep. I looked back to the window, trying to judge how early it was by the amount of sunlight streaming in. How long had we slept?

Daniel shifted in his chair, eyes opening, indigo gaze meeting mine. His hair was rumpled, making my fingers itch to smooth it down. He sat up straight, stretching with his arms above his head, making his shirt pull up. My eyes were riveted to the tanned skin his movements revealed, the muscled planes of his lower stomach and the strip of hair travelling down below the waistband of his jeans.

He dropped his arms and I turned away, a deep blush sweeping over my face. My entire body felt flushed with heat, and I ducked my head, grabbing the end of my plait and tugging off the rubber band. I finger combed my hair loose, using it as a shield while I struggled to regain my composure.

'What time is it?' Daniel got to his feet.

He gave a soft sigh, the sound of it setting a shiver over my body. I peeked through my hair, drinking in the sight of him as he stretched again, torso pushing forward, hands pressed into the small of his back. I didn't realise I hadn't answered his question until he faced me straight on and called my name.

'Ah, I don't know. I just woke up.'

He yawned, hand coming up to cover his mouth. 'We'd better wake the others. We need to get out of here before the owners turn up.'

I brushed my hair back from my face and got off the bed,

doing my best to smooth the covers as he moved over to wake Angel. His voice was gentle, soothing, and I lost myself in the sound as he murmured quietly to his sister. Then he left the room to go in search of Andie and Nick.

Angel's hair was a tangled mess, having been loose when she went to sleep. After she had tidied up the bed she'd slept in, I helped her to untangle it as best we could before she twisted it up into a knot at the nape of her neck. After a quick trip to the main bathroom, I headed into the kitchen to find the others gathered there. Angel soon joined us, and all eyes went to her.

'Do we have time for breakfast?' Andie asked, a wide yawn muffling her words.

Angel shook her head, screwing up her face. 'I don't know. I'm sorry. I'm still not able to sense anything.'

'I don't think we should risk it,' I said. 'We have no idea when the owners will turn up. We should get out of here while it's still early and traffic will be light.'

'Besides,' said Nick, 'there's no coffee here, remember.' He nudged Andie with his elbow. 'Breakfast without coffee is just torture.'

Andie gave him a smile. 'That's it. We are blowing this joint.'

After a quick tidy up, we piled into the 4WD once Nick backed it out of the shed. Daniel rode shotgun, with Andie, Angel and me in the back. I was once again barefoot, as we had return all the items we'd borrowed the night before. With luck, the owners would never know anyone had been in their house.

Nick carefully reversed out of the yard, but stopped before backing onto the road. 'Where to now?'

Daniel and Andie offered up suggestions while I remained silent, lack of memories putting me at a distinct disadvantage. Angel also didn't contribute, which was understandable seeing as she had spent the last fifteen years locked away at the Wood Estate. It would be up to the others to decide our path.

Not that it really mattered.

Without proof to show to the police, we were only delaying the inevitable. Sooner or later we would run out of places to hide, and the police would find us. Angel, Andie and I would be taken back to the estate to be tortured and experimented on by the woman who claimed to be my mother, while Nick and Daniel would go to jail for daring to help us.

I gave a sigh, and Daniel twisted around to face me. 'It will be okay,' he said. 'We'll find somewhere where you'll be safe.'

I shook my head, giving him a sad smile. 'We'll never be safe. With proof, we stood a chance of getting the police to believe us. Without it, we have nothing.'

'Why don't we wait and see what's on the disks Andie found before we throw in the towel,' he said, a teasing light in his eyes.

'Disks? What disks?' My voice rose as I looked over to her. 'You found disks?'

She grinned at me, nodding. 'Yep, in the back section of the torture chamber, while you were reuniting with Mummy Dearest. She had them locked away in a safe, but Angel managed to get it open.' She reached down and picked up a plastic bag that had been shoved down on the floor at her feet, and handed it over to me.

I opened it, anticipation making me twitch as I put my hand inside and pulled out one of the disks. Angel's full name and the date the footage was filmed were neatly printed on a label stuck to the front of the case, along with the words "Subject A". I delved into the bag, coming up with over two dozen disks in all, most of them with Angel's name on them, but a couple with mine. They weren't the only things in the bag.

I reached back in and pulled out the folder I had taken from Dr Wood's desk.

My folder.

I met Daniel's gaze. I hadn't realised he'd still had it on him when we'd fled the estate.

'We haven't looked inside,' he said. 'It's your file. Your life.' He pointed at the bag of disks. 'Nick told me about those after we got home. You girls were exhausted, already asleep. We figured it would be better to wait until morning when we could all look at them together.'

It was an effort to relax my fingers, to not scrunch the folder into a ball and throw it out the window. Did I want to know what it contained? What if it confirmed what Dr Wood had said, that she was my mother and I was mentally ill?

I shoved the folder back in with the disks and dropped the bag to the floor beside my feet. Then I lifted my head and forced myself to smile at Daniel, face feeling frozen. 'Thank you,' I said. 'For everything.'

He gave a slight nod, and faced the front as Nick finally pulled out onto the road. I had no idea where we were going, having somehow missed the naming of our destination while engrossed with the contents of the plastic bag. I should have felt happy, relieved we might have the proof we needed, but all I could think about was what might be in the folder.

What secrets about my past did it reveal?

Did I really want to know?

Minutes later Nick pulled up in front of a small cottage. It looked out of place in a street that appeared to have been redeveloped with mini mansions squeezed onto the blocks either side of it. A path, trimmed with neat flower beds, led to the front door. The door itself was open, with a security screen blocking access.

'You guys wait here,' said Andie, as she unclipped her seat belt and opened the door.

'You're sure Mr Simpson will help us?' Daniel asked.

Andie shrugged. 'We have nowhere else to go, and he did ask us to bring Angel to visit him.' She climbed out of the car and we watched as she walked up to the front door and knocked on the screen.

'Angel came here, last time she escaped from the estate,' said Nick. 'Those orderlies found her and dragged her back, and the old guy has been worried about her ever since. When we came looking for her, he realised Andie was her identical twin and told us what happened. That's how we knew for sure she was still alive, and where to start looking for her.'

I watched as an old man with a walking frame appeared on the other side of the screen. It was hard to tell from this distance, but he appeared to be pleased to see her, and quickly opened the screen door. After a brief conversation, Andie hurried back to the car.

'He said we can hide the 4WD in his garage. He hasn't driven a car for years so it's empty.' She indicated for Angel and me to get out of the vehicle. I scooped up the bag containing my file and the disks and followed her down the path, to where the old man held the screen door open for us, tears streaming down his face as he looked at Angel.

'Oh, my dear, you don't know how good it is to see you,' he said to her as he backed up to allow us to enter his house. 'And to see you reunited with your family, it truly is marvellous.' He kept talking about how happy this made him, voice choked with tears, as he led us into his tiny lounge room. Daniel and Nick soon joined us, filling the small space to capacity.

I still held the bag of disks, not sure what to do with it. Mr Simpson didn't appear to have a television let alone a DVD player we could view the disks on. Before I could ask him if he had a computer, he shuffled out of the room, calling for Andie and Angel to come and help him in the kitchen.

The rest of us took a seat, Daniel beside me on a brocade two-seater sofa, with Nick taking the matching one directly opposite.

A steady murmur of voices came from the kitchen, and soon Angel and Andie returned to the lounge, carrying trays of food and drink. The enticing scent of coffee and toast filled the small room. Mr Simpson followed, huffing quietly as he twisted his walking frame around, so he could take a seat in an armchair.

Angel and Andie placed their trays on the small coffee table and then squeezed onto the sofa with Nick. The next few minutes were filled with steady munching. I was surprised to find I had an appetite. Perhaps hunger was overriding my stress levels. I had no idea how long it had been since I'd eaten anything, making me just as keen as the others to polish off the pile of toast.

Once my stomach was full, I relaxed back in my seat, sipping my coffee, as Nick and Daniel fought over the last piece of toast. I felt replete; at ease. I looked down at the plastic bag near my feet, briefly contemplating opening it and taking out the file with my name on it. Then again, maybe I should enjoy this moment of peace for as long as I could. Something was sure to upset the equilibrium soon enough.

I smiled when Daniel managed to score the last piece of toast. He leaned back, shoulder bumping mine, the rest of him pressing against my side. I wanted to slide even closer to him, rest my head on his broad shoulder, but resisted the urge.

Instead I watched the people who had somehow become vitally important to me in such a short time. I didn't think it was just because of the situation we were all in, or that they were the only people I knew in the world.

We were connected in a much deeper way than mere

proximity could explain.

I sighed, and reflected on how lucky I had been to find them. Then again, maybe it hadn't been luck. Maybe it was meant to be. I looked at Andie and Nick, cuddled together on the other couch. They'd only known each other a couple of days and yet it was clear they were made for each other. That wasn't to say I thought Daniel and I were also fated to be a couple, but the possibility of seeing where the feelings I was sure were blooming between us filled me with a sense of rightness.

Andie asked Mr Simpson if he had a computer, dragging my thoughts back to the here and now.

As she followed his directions to find his laptop and set it up, my stomach churned, making me regret eating so much.

This was it.

This was when we would finally discover the truth about what Dr Wood had done to us.

11

Tears streamed down my face as I watched the recorded vision of Angel as a child of eight or nine being forced to perform. Dr Wood held up a card, with the back to Angel so she couldn't see the symbol on the other side, demanding the little girl tell her what she "saw". Each time Angel failed to scribble the correct answer on the whiteboard clutched in her tiny hands, Dr Wood produced a slim black device which she used to administer a localised electric shock.

The young Angel on the screen valiantly fought to hold back tears as she recovered and focused on the card in Dr Wood's hand. The next time her answer was correct, but she received no praise. All she got was the selection of a new card and a repeat of the test until the number of times she got it wrong far outweighed the number of correct answers.

Exhausted, barely able to lift her head, Angel made no sign of protest as the brutish orderly we had encountered the night before scooped her up and placed her on a bed. Dr Wood produced a syringe and injected some substance into Angel's arm. Then the screen went black.

I looked over to Angel, wrapped in her sister's arms, tears running down both their cheeks. How had she remained sane, after everything she had endured? There were well over a dozen tapes with her name on them, dated over the last fifteen years.

'I knew Andie would come for me.' Angel's voice whispered through my mind. 'I just had to hold on, to never give up hope I would be free.'

I wiped my cheeks, giving her a watery smile as Daniel

reached over to enfold me in his arms. I didn't resist, snuggling in, fortifying myself with the feel of him, the warmth and strength he radiated so naturally. With his help, I would be able to endure whatever happened next.

After prompting from a silent Andie, Nick pulled another disk from the bag and set it to play. I stiffened, recognising my name on the label. Daniel's arms tightened around me.

'Are you sure about this? We don't have to watch it,' he murmured in my ear.

'Yes, I do. I need to see what she did to me.'

His arms tightened around me as the disk played. Dr Wood appeared first and dispassionately stated my name as Subject C, followed by the date and time. I frowned. The date she'd given was over a year ago. But how could that be? I'd thought I'd only been at the estate for a few months at the most.

How long had I been there?

I forgot about questions of time as the view shifted to show me, strapped to the bed in the lower treatment room. I was wearing a yellow sundress, hair loose around my shoulders as I struggled against the straps.

'Please, Mum. Don't do this. I'll sign the money over to you, I promise. As soon as I turn eighteen and the trust is in my name, you can have every last cent.' Eyes rimmed red and wide with fear, face blotchy from crying, I continued to beg and plead for her to stop as she ordered the large orderly to pin my head in place. Then she secured a strap to keep it immobile.

Once that was done, the orderly let go and Dr Wood placed electrodes on both of my temples. Without saying a word or even looking in my direction, she rolled the trolley with the ECT machine on it closer to the bed, connecting wires to the electrodes and adjusting dials. Finally, once she was satisfied with the setup, she leaned over me, the camera catching the cool expression in her eyes.

'Well then, let's see if you can't be of some use to me after all. I need a test subject to contrast the data I have complied on Subject A. As I am one hundred percent certain you have no measurable talent, you will be the perfect addition to my studies. When I show them how utterly ordinary you are, my peers will be able to see just how extraordinary Subject A is.'

'Subject A?' My voice in the recording quavered, eyes darting to the ECT machine and back to Dr Wood. Even though I had just heard myself call her Mum, I could never think of her that way. She was a monster. She would never be my mother.

Her eyes lit up as she said, 'Subject A is the lynchpin of my research, her psychic abilities irrefutable. I'd introduce the two of you, but I'm afraid that could pollute the data. Better to keep you as far away from one another as possible. Besides, she'll have company soon enough, once I finally get my hands on her sister.'

Now her eyes held a cruel light as she looked at me. 'No company for you though. Now I've found the right leverage to persuade Dr Chandler to sign the papers to have you committed, it would be best if people forget you even exist.'

I shuddered to see the relish in her eyes as she told the past version of me just how alone I was. The outright terror in my eyes as she shoved a gag into my mouth was painful to watch, but I couldn't tear my eyes away as she then switched on the ECT machine and sent a torrent of volts into my body. I whimpered in sympathy, an echo of half-remembered pain flooding through me, ducking my head and burying my face into Daniel's shoulder.

'That's enough,' he said, voice hoarse as he cradled me in his arms. 'Turn it off. That should be plenty of evidence to convince the police to have that woman arrested and the estate

199

shut down.'

No one argued with him, Nick quickly hitting the stop button.

We sat in silence for a long moment, staring at the blank screen.

It was Mr Simpson who finally broke the silence.

'I knew it was bad, whatever they were doing to you. But I had no idea ...' He shook his head, tears shining in his eyes as he looked at Angel. 'It's immoral, how anybody could do that to an innocent child.' He then looked over to me. 'And you, poor girl, to have a mother like that. I can't imagine how you must feel, to be betrayed by the person who should have done everything in her power to protect you. It's just wrong.'

He took in a deep breath. 'The police need to see this. They need to see what that horrible woman has been doing to you. She must be stopped, and held accountable for her crimes.'

'That's the plan,' said Daniel, determination in his voice. 'Once they're through with her, she'll never be able to hurt Celeste and Angel, or anyone else, ever again. I'll make sure of it.'

He gently untangled his arms from around me and stood. 'I'll hand the disks over to the police. Until we're sure they understand exactly what's been going on, we can't risk them knowing where Celeste is. Angel and Andie need to remain hidden as well, in case Dr Wood has told the police about them.'

I stood up. 'What if the police arrest you for helping me? Dr Wood said you and Nick would go to jail.'

He gave me a confident smile and cupped my face in his hand, long fingers stroking my cheekbone. 'You don't need to worry about me.'

I put my hand over his, a sinking feeling in the pit of my stomach. 'I don't like the idea of you going to the police on your own.'

He leaned forward, brushing his lips against mine. 'I'll be fine.'

Lips tingling from the brief kiss, I stared at Daniel, wanting to latch on to him and never let go.

'I'll go with him,' said Nick.

'Great. Then they can arrest both of you. Awesome,' said Andie, her expression troubled.

'I'll go. They have no reason to arrest me. Only, I'm going to need a ride.' Mr Simpson shrugged apologetically. 'Had to hand my driver's licence in three years ago.'

Despite my and Andie's objections, Nick and Daniel soon piled into the borrowed 4WD with Mr Simpson. I couldn't sit still, bursting with nervous energy, so I cleared away the breakfast dishes while Andie filled the kitchen sink with hot soapy water. I washed, while Andie dried, and Angel put everything away.

With the three of us working together, the house was tidied up sooner than I would have liked, leaving me restless and on edge. I wandered back into the lounge room, looking for something to do. My eyes fell on the brown folder.

I stared at it, not sure I was ready to discover what it contained. But I had nothing else with which to occupy my time, and sitting around wondering what was happening at the police station would just tangle me up in knots. I scooped up the folder and headed to the small dining room, aware of Angel and Andie hovering silently behind me as I opened it and spread the papers it contained over the table. With a deep breath, I picked up the first piece of paper and scanned the contents.

It was my birth certificate, stating in black and white that I was the daughter of Joanna and Phillip Wood. My full name was Celeste Maree Wood, and I had recently turned nineteen. The second form was a letter dated shortly before I turned eighteen, signed by Dr Evan Chandler, who advised I was suffering severe mental issues and needed to be hospitalised for my own safety.

I tossed it aside and perused a pile of documents stapled together, frowning as their meaning sank in. From what I understood, my father had died when I was a baby. He had left me a sizeable amount of money, set up in a trust fund. My mother was the sole executor for the fund until I turned eighteen.

This was the money I had promised to give her in the footage.

Bank statements were included in the pile of papers, showing large withdrawals over the years, along with invoices and receipts from a range of companies. I flicked through them, anger flaring as I realised what they meant.

'She used my money to build the Wood Estate.'

Andie crowded closer and I handed her the stack of papers.

'It all came from a trust fund my father set up when I was born. She had control of it until I turned eighteen. That's why she had me committed, so I wouldn't stop her stealing all my money. I was never crazy.'

'Of course you weren't crazy. She's the crazy one,' said Andie as she perused the documents, shaking her head. 'I knew she was a cold-hearted bitch, but to think she would do that to her own daughter. I don't have words for how monstrous she is.'

Angel placed a hand on my arm. 'I'm so sorry, Celeste. I know you were hoping to find your family, as I did. But you aren't alone. We're your family now.'

She was right. I'd still held out hope that somewhere there was a family looking for me, missing me. But my father was long dead, a large portion of the inheritance he left me used to fund the torture of myself and Angel. I could be bitter about that, or I could accept the facts and move on.

I turned to Angel and gave her a grateful smile. 'Thank you, for everything.'

She smiled back, and I basked in the knowledge my new family would never let me down. Together we would handle the fallout of the investigation sure to be launched once Mr Simpson handed our evidence to the police. With Dr Wood behind bars and the institution she had stolen my inheritance to build closed down, we would all get a chance to live a normal and happy life.

My smile widened sure that Daniel was going to be a huge part of that life.

Everything was going to be okay.

I had no memories of my past, but my future was going to be amazing.

I just knew it.

12

Angel's warning sounded in my head a split second before a loud knock sounded on the front door.

'It's them.' Face pale, she clutched Andie's arm. 'They found us.'

I got up, knocking over the chair in my haste. The thump as it hit the tiled floor sounded impossibly loud. Whoever was at the front door had to have heard the bang.

Sure enough, the knock came again. 'Mr Simpson, this is the Easton Police. We need to talk to you, to discuss an urgent matter.'

I shared a startled glance with the others. Was it Mr Simpson the police were here to see after all? Perhaps their appearance on the doorstep had nothing to do with us.

'What do we do?' I whispered.

'We leave. We can't risk it.' Andie spun around, looking for the back door. But the way the cottage was set up meant the hallway ran right through the house. To get to the back door, we would be exposed to the view of whoever was at the front door. The screen door was locked, but the front door itself was wide open.

We were trapped.

'I'll go and see what they want,' said Andie, rolling her shoulders back. 'You two wait here, out of sight.'

Angel and I gave quick nods as Andie stepped into the hall and moved towards the front door. We got as close as we could to the hall, so we could listen in without being seen.

'Can I help you, officer?' Andie's voice was cool, sparking admiration for her courage. There was no way I could have sounded so calm if it had been me facing the police.

'I'm looking for Peter Simpson. Is he home?'

'Sorry, no. He went out a little while ago. Can I take a message?'

'And you are …?'

'His granddaughter.' A long silence met Andie's lie, and I tensed as I waited to see if she would be called on it.

'Do you know when your grandfather will be coming home? I'd really like to speak to him in person.'

'I'm afraid not. He had a few errands to run, so he could be a while.'

'I was given to understand Mr Simpson doesn't have a driver's licence. Must be hard for him to run errands when he would have to rely on public transport. Expensive too.'

'My brother, his grandson, is driving him. We like to help out whenever we can.'

'That's very good of you. Or would be, if he were actually your grandfather.'

'What? Of course he's my grandfather. Why else would I be here?' Andie's voice shook, giving away the lie.

Heart pounding, I turned to Angel, reaching out to her with my hand. She clutched mine and we raced into the hall, calling for Andie to run.

A thud came from the back of the house, the screen door rattling as it was kicked in. A second police officer appeared in the doorway, blocking our escape. Andie whirled to face us.

I reached deep within myself to call the lightning.

'No,' Angel said in my head, tightening her grip on my hand. 'We can't use our powers. They're innocent. We could hurt them.'

I sagged, letting go of the burgeoning energy I had harnessed, realising she was right.

'Open this door, right now.'

Andie stiffened at the command from the first officer, but did unlock the screen door. He stalked inside, looming over her. She backed up until she reached my side, the three of us presenting a unified front. The officer who had kept us occupied at the front while his younger partner sneaked around the back, was middle aged, dark hair liberally splashed with grey. His eyes were deep-set, making it appear as if he wore a permanent scowl.

His eyes were hard as he looked over us, wary, as if he expected us to make a dash for freedom at any moment. Not that I wasn't tempted, but I was smart enough to realise the odds were against us. He ushered us into the lounge, getting us to take a seat as his partner searched the rest of the house.

The younger officer soon returned and the two of them moved into the hallway to have a private conversation.

'Can you hear what they're saying?' I asked Angel, tapping the side of my head.

'It doesn't work that way,' she said, screwing up her mouth. 'I can't hear anyone else's thoughts, only yours and Andie's.'

We sat in ignorance until both police officers returned and stared at us.

The older one looked from Angel to Andie. 'Now then, which one of you is Angela Sherman and which one is Andrea?'

'I'm Andie. This is my sister, Angel.' She stressed the names.

The officer grimaced but didn't respond as his gaze slid to me. 'And you're Celeste Wood.'

The ball of dread in my stomach had grown heavier with each name he uttered. There was no way we were going to be able to bluff our way out of this mess.

'So then, which one of you is going to tell me what

you've done with Mr Simpson?'

I shared puzzled glances with Andie and Angel, shaking my head. 'I don't understand. We haven't done anything to him. He was on his way to the police station with...'

He stiffened. 'With who?' He looked to Andie. 'Your brother?'

She nodded, and his frown intensified. 'Why was your brother taking Mr Simpson to the station? What's going on here?'

Andie looked at me and Angel, her expression clearly asking what we should do. I gave her a shrug, figuring we should tell the truth. As Angel had no voice, it would have to come from me.

I sat up straight, and looked the officer in the eye. 'He was handing in evidence, to show you what happened to us while we were imprisoned at the Wood Estate.'

'Imprisoned.' His eyebrows rose.

'Yes. Imprisoned, and tortured. Dr Wood filmed us while she electrocuted Angel and me. We found the disks, and Mr Simpson was taking them to the police station, so she can be arrested.'

'Now, hang on just a minute. You were all patients at the Wood Estate. Dr Wood reported the three of you as missing. Now you're telling me she electrocuted you.' His eyebrows rose even higher. 'And isn't she your mother?'

'According to my birth certificate, but after what she did to me ...' I shook my head. 'She's a monster.'

He ran a hand through his hair, looking over to his partner for a moment, and then back to us. 'You say you have evidence. Disks.'

'Yes. Mr Simpson has them.'

'So, there's none here?'

I shook my head, and then jumped when Angel clamped a hand on my arm, her expression brightening as she pointed to the laptop. 'Nick didn't take the last disk,' she said in my head.

The younger officer moved over to the laptop. 'Don't touch it,' said his partner. 'That's potential evidence.'

I felt a tingle in my arm where Angel touched me, and then warmth in the air around us as she used her powers to bring the laptop out of sleep mode. Within seconds the screen had come to life.

Both officers stiffened, hands going to their holsters. Then they froze as the footage of my first session with Dr Wood played.

'What the hell,' said the younger officer, stepping closer to the laptop.

'There are documents on the kitchen table, receipts and other stuff that prove Dr Wood has been stealing Celeste's money for years,' said Andie. 'She had her falsely committed so she didn't lose access to her trust fund once Celeste turned eighteen.'

When the footage ended, the senior officer glanced over at us, sympathy and concern in his expression. And something else. Regret.

A knock at the front door made his expression switch to one of guilt. He shifted his feet, a grimace on his lips as he sent his partner to the front door.

'I'm sorry,' he said, voice low. 'I had to call it in, that we'd found you. I didn't know.'

'Didn't know wh–'

'Hello, girls.'

Shock stole my breath as Dr Wood entered the lounge room, with five orderlies at her back, three of which I had never seen before.

I shot to my feet, Andie and Angel joining me.

'My men and I can take care of things from here, thank you, officers,' said Dr Wood, giving the senior officer a cool smile. 'The sooner I get the young ladies back to the estate, the quicker I can see that their mental states have not been adversely affected by their little excursion.'

'We are not going anywhere with you,' said Andie. She faced the officers. 'You saw what she did to Celeste. You need to arrest her, right now.'

'There's no need to be so melodramatic, Andrea. The officer isn't going to arrest me. I'm not the one in the wrong here.'

'I wouldn't be too sure about that,' said the officer, turning to face her. 'Seems you have some explaining to do. How about we move this down to the station, where you can explain to me how electrocuting a young woman is a viable treatment option.'

Dr Wood's cool smile wavered for a second. 'I can assure you, electro convulsive therapy is a perfectly legal and widely used form of treatment for those with severe mental illness. While it might appear to be torture to the layman, I was in fact trying to help my daughter.'

'Blackmailing another doctor so you can continue to have access to her trust fund; is that a perfectly legal and widely used form of treatment as well?'

I couldn't contain my grin as the officer moved towards her. 'Dr Wood, you're under arrest for–'

Everything happened so fast, it was hard to believe my eyes as the five orderlies jumped forward at a sharp command from Dr Wood. They each produced a syringe, two of them darting forward to jab the police officers in the arm, while the other three made for Andie, Angel and me. In the cramped lounge room, with so many people crammed into it, there was precious little space for manoeuvring.

My arm was caught in a punishing grip, a sharp sting flaring on my shoulder as I struggled to call on my strange ability. But whatever was in the syringe quickly spread through my body, making me light headed. The small amount of energy I had managed to call fizzled out. It was getting harder to keep my eyes open. I fought to stay conscious, head flopping, horror gripping me at the sight of the two police officers falling to the ground.

'You'll never get away with this,' I said, words slurring as I sought to focus on Dr Wood. 'The police are going to come after you.'

She gave me a chilling smile as she stepped over to where her orderly held me upright. She gripped my face in cruel hands. 'I'd be more concerned about my own future, if I were you. Once I have the three of you back at the estate, and go public with my findings, no one will be able to touch me. I'm going to be the most influential scientist in the world.'

She let go and my head fell forward, eyes closing. And there was nothing I could do to stop it.

13

The orderly scooped me off my feet as darkness threatened to sweep me away completely. I fought to hold on, sinking my consciousness deep within myself to search for the faint spark of energy I had called on before.

A trace of light sparked in the darkness. I focused on it, pulling it closer to me, willing it to brighten. My body began to tingle as the light slowly spread, warming every part of me. Soon it was uncomfortably warm, and I felt myself sweating as I was laid on a hard, cool surface. My body was jostled, and I had a sense of Andie and Angel on either side of me.

I wriggled until I was touching them, sending the energy I had managed to harness into their bodies as well, instinctively using it to burn away whatever drug was in our systems. The process was slow, agonisingly so, but soon the fog weighing down my thoughts lifted. I could sit up, keeping a hand on each twin, as I focused on clearing the last trace of the drug from their bodies.

They groaned as they rolled onto their sides before sitting up. We faced one another in the gloom of the van we'd been tossed into.

'Are you ready for this?' I asked.

They both gave me firm nods, and I urged them to brace themselves as I placed my hands on the floor of the van, closing my eyes as I sent a bolt of lightning into the vehicle.

Sparks flared around us as the energy I had summoned travelled towards the engine, targeting the battery, causing it to immediately lose power.

Shouts sounded from the front of the van as it lost

momentum, slowing gradually.

I moved to the rear door of the van, gripping the handle. It was locked, but one short sharp burst of lightning forced it open. The door swung wide with the movement of the vehicle, and I looked out to see Dr Wood glaring at me from the front passenger seat of a large sedan close behind. I sent out another bolt of lightning, targeting the engine of the sedan as the van came to a final stop.

Dr Wood's car skidded to a halt.

Angel, Andie and I scrambled from the rear of the van, and I tensed as I saw we were on the long driveway that led to the Wood Estate. Car doors opened as Dr Wood and the orderlies got out of their vehicle and ran toward us.

I gripped Angel and Andie's hands, pulling them to the left, trying to keep Dr Wood and the orderlies in front of us. But they quickly spread out to encircle us, though they kept a wary distance as they blocked off any avenue of escape.

We would have to fight our way free.

I risked a quick glance at Angel, receiving a determined nod in return.

We would not let them take us.

Time to show Dr Wood exactly what we were capable of.

We shifted so Andie was in the middle, leaving Angel and me each with a hand free. Angel pointed at the ground and a wall of fire sprang up at her command, forming a wide circle around us. The heat from the flames seared my skin, and then Angel waved her hand. I felt a pull in my head as the flames twisted before spreading out in an almost vertical arc, the heat from the blaze now pushing away from us.

The crackle and sizzle of the flames was the only sound as Dr Wood and the orderlies backed away, hands over their faces to shield themselves from the heat. The brutish orderly ran back to the van and leaned in through the driver's side. When he straightened up he had a cruel smirk on his face and a small fire extinguisher in his hand.

He got it working and sprayed it on the nearest section of the flames. Angel worked to renew the blaze, the rush of her power making my body tingle each time, but as soon as she got the blaze going again he would dart in and extinguish it.

Through the flames I caught a glimpse of Dr Wood talking on her mobile phone, no doubt calling for reinforcements. We couldn't wait for them to arrive with more extinguishers. Angel's ability to create fire was already fading, even with Andie lending her strength. I could feel a lessening in the brush of it against my skin.

I had to do something.

Dark clouds were forming in the air above us, hinting at a possible storm to come.

I narrowed my eyes and focused on the darkest of the clouds, calling on the energy coursing through my body. When I held all I could, I pointed at the cloud and set my lightning free.

It hit the cloud, setting off a heavy rumble, flashes of lightning flaring in the dark grey depths.

I crooked my fingers, calling the lightning to me. It came eagerly, heading straight for me.

At the last minute I pulled my hand down and pointed at the ground in front of Dr Wood. The lightning speared the dirt, followed by a concussive blast that knocked her and the orderlies off their feet. They flew backwards, landing on their backs as a shower of dirt rained down on them.

My ears buzzed, body swaying, though my ability appeared to protect the twins and me from the worst effects. I prepared to call the lightning again, pointing up at the cloud, ready to bring down another strike.

Dr Wood scrambled to her feet, hands over her ears, face a twisted mask of rage. 'Don't think this will stop me for long,' she shouted as the orderlies also got to their feet, some of them shaking their heads.

Her gaze moved to Angel and Andie. 'The three of you belong to me.'

I didn't bother replying, ready to send another bolt of lightning her way if she came any closer, as Angel renewed her efforts with fire.

The ground beneath our feet rocked, causing all of us to stumble. I gasped, wide-eyed as I looked around me. The rush of power had not come from me or Angel. It came from farther down the driveway.

Shock flooded through my mind, broadcast by Angel. Her fire faltered as she looked toward the estate, the source of the mini quake.

I called out to her as the orderlies took advantage of her distraction to move closer. At my mental shake, she refocused, and her ring of fire flared up again.

The wail of multiple sirens sounded in the distance, and the brutish orderly latched on to Dr Wood's arm, tugging her back towards her car. I sent the bolt of lightning I had harnessed over their heads, letting it slam into the car, determined not to let them get away. I did the same to the van, immobilising it in a shower of sparks.

Just before the first police car rounded the corner into the driveway, I urged Angel to let go of her fire. It would be hard enough explaining what had happened here without the police bearing witness to what we could do.

I heard a sigh and turned around as Angel collapsed into Andie's arms. Andie didn't look to be in much better shape and I battled my own exhaustion as I crouched beside them. Vision hazy, I watched as the police pulled up and jumped out of their vehicles, taking the situation in with hard glances.

I forced my eyes to stay open as one of the police officers went up to Dr Wood, a set of handcuffs in his hands.

I let out a low sigh.

It was over.

We were safe.

She couldn't hurt us anymore.

I slumped over, arms around Angel and Andie, and let unconsciousness take me.

14

I came to with a start, sitting upright, and gasped.

I was in a hospital bed, the metal sides up to stop me from rolling out in my sleep. I looked down and saw I was wearing a green hospital-issue gown. I scanned the rest of the room in a panic, terrified I was back at the estate.

My gaze settled on Daniel, sleeping in an uncomfortable position on an old brown armchair in the corner closet to the bed. He was wearing the same clothes as last time I'd seen him, a faint hint of a five o'clock shadow on his chin.

As if he felt the weight of my gaze, he opened his eyes and gave me a smile that set my pulse pounding and created a flight of butterflies in my stomach.

'Hey,' he said, as he stretched and slowly got to his feet. He came to the edge of the bed, reaching out a hand to smooth a tangle of hair back from my face. 'Good to see you're awake, finally. Thought you were pulling a Sleeping Beauty and I was going to have to kiss you to get you to wake up.'

If I thought my pulse had been pounding before, it was nothing compared to what it did now at the thought of him kissing me. My eyes went wide, and I caught my breath, unable to look away as he stared at me.

'Hey, don't panic. I was just joking.' He frowned when I continued to stare at him without saying a word.

Heat suffused my face. Of course he was joking. I was so stupid, thinking he was as interested in me as I was in him. I looked away, unable to bear being so exposed.

'Celeste, look at me,' he said, hand moving to my chin and gently turning my head, so I was facing him. 'When I do kiss you, it won't be when you're unconscious.'

'Wait …what …? Does that mean you do want to kiss me?' I inwardly cringed at the way I stumbled over the words, but this time I was not looking away, searching his eyes for answers.

'Are you kidding me? I've been wanting to kiss you so badly, ever since I realised what an amazing person you are. But I didn't want to scare you off.'

A hint of nervousness entered his eyes as he straightened up and cleared his throat. 'That is, if you want me to kiss you. I mean, I understand if you're not interested. We've been through a lot the last couple of days. I don't want to pressure you into a relationship or anything. I was just thinking we could spend some time together, just you and me, get to know each other better.'

'Yes.'

'Yes, I'm pressuring you? Yes, you want to spend time with me? Or yes, you want me to kiss you?'

I gave him a shy smile. 'I would love to spend time with you.'

He grinned back at me and I gave a happy sigh. Everything was going to work out just fine.

Then, a frown furrowed my brow as I remembered what had been happening before I collapsed.

'Angel and Andie? Are they okay?'

Daniel sat on the edge of the bed, taking my hand in his and giving it a reassuring squeeze. 'They're fine. They woke up a couple of hours ago and were released. Nick took them home. That's the good news.'

I tensed. 'And the bad news?'

'Dr Wood was arrested, back at the estate, but then some hotshot lawyer turned up and got her and the orderlies released on some technicality.'

My hand tightened on his as he continued to talk.

'By the time the police had got new paperwork and returned to the estate to arrest them again, she and that big orderly had vanished. One of the patients is missing too; Ethan something. The police can't be sure if he took advantage of the confusion to run off on his own or if he's with the others.'

Ethan? He might be the one I'd encountered, the one I had knocked out with my powers before I had control of them.

'But you don't need to worry about any of that anymore. The police are searching for them, and they're bound to catch up with them sooner or later. All you have to concentrate on is getting released from this hospital, so you can come home with me and the girls, where you belong.'

Home.

With Daniel and the others.

I liked the sound of that.

I mustered up a smile, pushing away my worry about Dr Wood and the missing patient. That was in the hands of the police.

It was time for me to start living my life, my way.

I still didn't remember my past but the future was opening up before me, and I was determined to make the most of it.

ACKNOWLEDGEMENTS

Writing a book may seem like a solitary endeavor, but there are a whole host of people who help turn an initial idea into a fully-fledged story. As always, my family and friends are there to support me as I hide away in my office playing with imaginary characters. Mum, Grant and my children, as well as Donna, Jennifer and Jael, are always there for me, and don't seem to mind the chaos that abounds when I'm in full-on creation mode and have neglected the housework.

Then there are the friends who are also writers who understand what I am talking about when I say I can't get a character to behave the way I want them to. They are there to offer advice when I need it, encouragement when my energy is flagging and to help me brainstorm when I have written my characters into a corner. Sandy Curtis and Sue-Ellen Pashley have helped to make my stories shine in more ways than one.

Sally Odgers edited my words and made them flow much smoother, while Mariah Sinclair designed the most beautiful book cover I have ever seen. Both of these ladies have helped to make my book something I can be proud of.

Lastly, thank you to the readers who enjoyed the original version of Angel Fire and asked for more. Arcane Awakenings would not exist if it wasn't for you, and it's not nagging if you tell me to hurry up and write more stories, DD Line.

ABOUT THE AUTHOR

Shelley Russell Nolan is an avid reader who began writing her own stories at sixteen. Her first completed manuscript featured brain eating aliens and a butt kicking teenage heroine. Since then she has spent her time creating fantasy worlds where death is only the beginning and even freaks can fall in love.

The first two books in her debut adult urban fantasy series, *Lost Reaper* and *Winged Reaper*, are published by Atlas Productions

Born in New Zealand, moving to Australia with her family when she was seven, Shelley currently lives in Central Queensland, Australia, with her husband and two young children. They share their home with two wrecking ball kitties, a deformed budgerigar and two dogs that are fairly normal as dogs go.

Shelley loves to hear from her readers so feel free to contact her on Facebook or leave a review on Amazon or Goodreads or on her website - shelleyrussellnolan.com

ALSO BY SHELLEY RUSSELL NOLAN

Lost Reaper
(Book One of the Reaper Series)

The first dead body I ever saw was my own.

For twenty-five year old Tyler Morgan, being murdered was easy. Easy in comparison with working for the Grim Reaper.

Jonathon Grimm may have brought her back from the dead in exchange for working as a reaper for her hometown, Easton, but she has to find his lost reaper before she can enjoy her second chance at life. Only … the lost reaper isn't actually lost. He has a new body and a new life and no intention of turning himself in, even if it means giving Tyler her life back.

Tyler begins the grisly task of reaping the souls of Easton's dead while searching for the reaper. He could be anyone – the intriguing detective, Sam Lockwood; the handsome, wealthy Chris Bradbury; or the serial killer stalking the women of Easton. Women who bear an uncanny resemblance to Tyler.

But what is the ancient secret, hidden from mankind, that has motivated Grimm to choose Tyler for the morbid task?

As the killer closes in and Grimm's deadline draws closer, Tyler discovers she is fighting a much bigger threat than the Grim Reaper and time is running out for everyone.

Winged Reaper
(Book Two of the Reaper Series)

Secrets, lies and the Grim Reaper: a recipe for disaster!

Twenty-five-year-old Tyler Morgan is only alive--technically reborn--because the Grim Reaper offered her a job. Now she has to find a way to stop her 'boss' from starting a war that threatens the survival of mankind.

Weak and in need of fresh souls, the Grim Reaper has sent his Wraiths to Tyler's hometown, Easton, and by the time he gets his fill, it could turn into a graveyard.

Tyler's resolve is tested when old secrets surface and a new betrayal has her questioning where her loyalties lie.

Supported by the intriguing detective, Sam Lockwood; the handsome, wealthy Chris Bradbury; and sources she never expected to come to her aid, Tyler must fight her way to the truth if she is ever to find the strength to harness the powers she has inherited, and vanquish the Grim Reaper forever.

Silver Reaper
(Book Three of the Reaper Series)

How far would you go to save those marked for Death?

When the call to reap uncovers a new threat to Easton and its inhabitants, Tyler is drawn back into a world she thought she'd left behind.

Forced to face her greatest fears, she seeks to uncover the identity of the rogue reaper murdering men employed by her former ally. But the search leads her to a conspiracy decades in the making.

With the line between friends and enemies blurring, Tyler begins to question her loyalties as she fights to stop the storm threatening to engulf Easton. But when the Grim Reaper offers the last hope, death might be the least of her problems.

Who can Tyler trust when even her allies want her dead?